MAGICAL DAWN

Hanna Karlzon

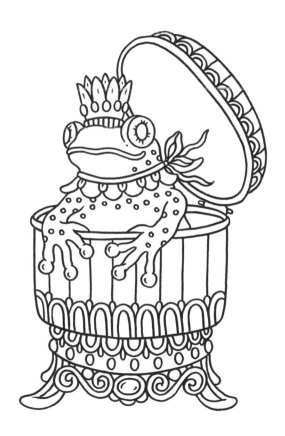

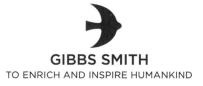

GIBBS SMITH
TO ENRICH AND INSPIRE HUMANKIND

26 25 24 23   11 10 9 8 7

Magical Dawn Coloring Book
Illustrations © 2017 Hanna Karlzon.

Gibbs Smith
P.O. Box 667
Layton, Utah 84041

1.800.835.4993 orders
www.gibbs-smith.com

ISBN: 978-1-4236-4659-4

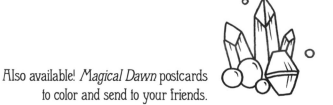

Also available! *Magical Dawn* postcards
to color and send to your friends.

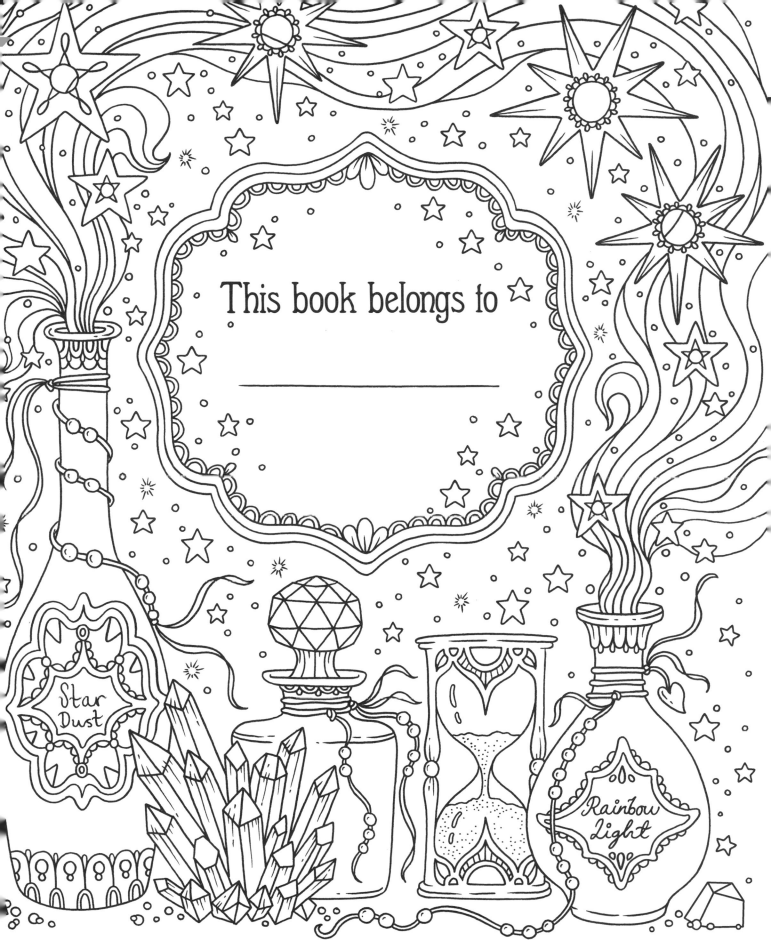

This book belongs to

_____

Star Dust

Rainbow Light

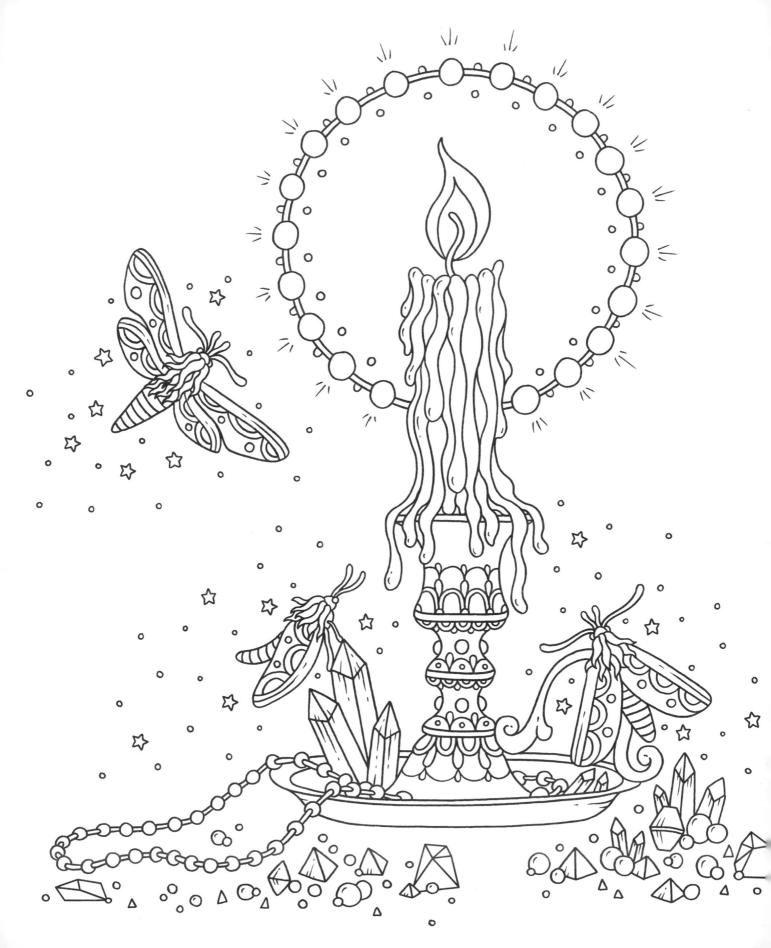

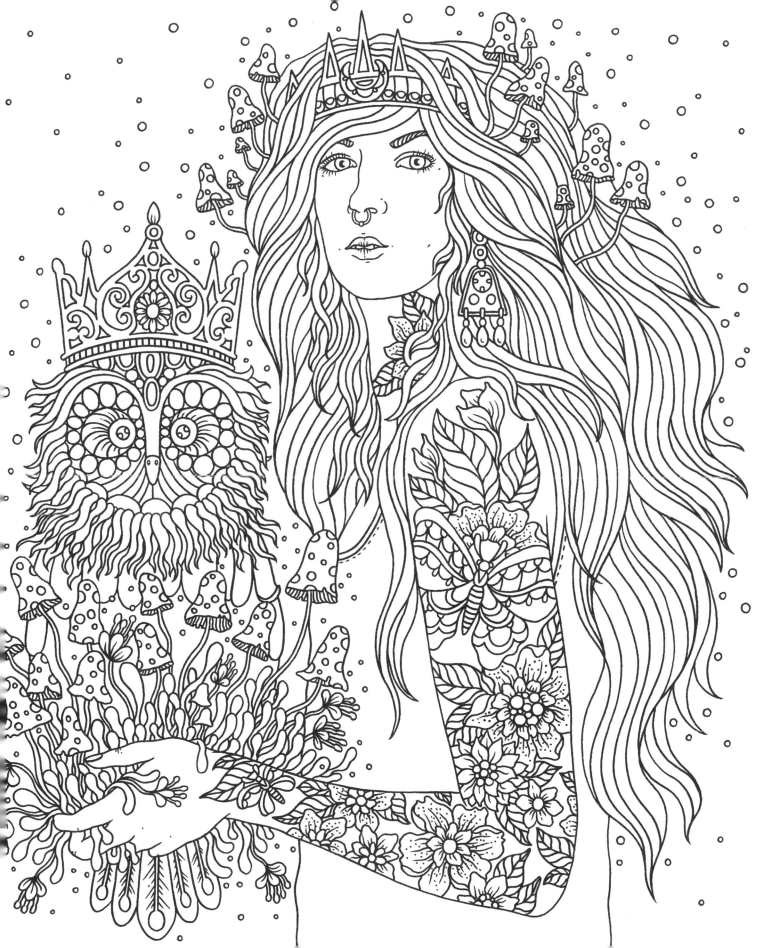

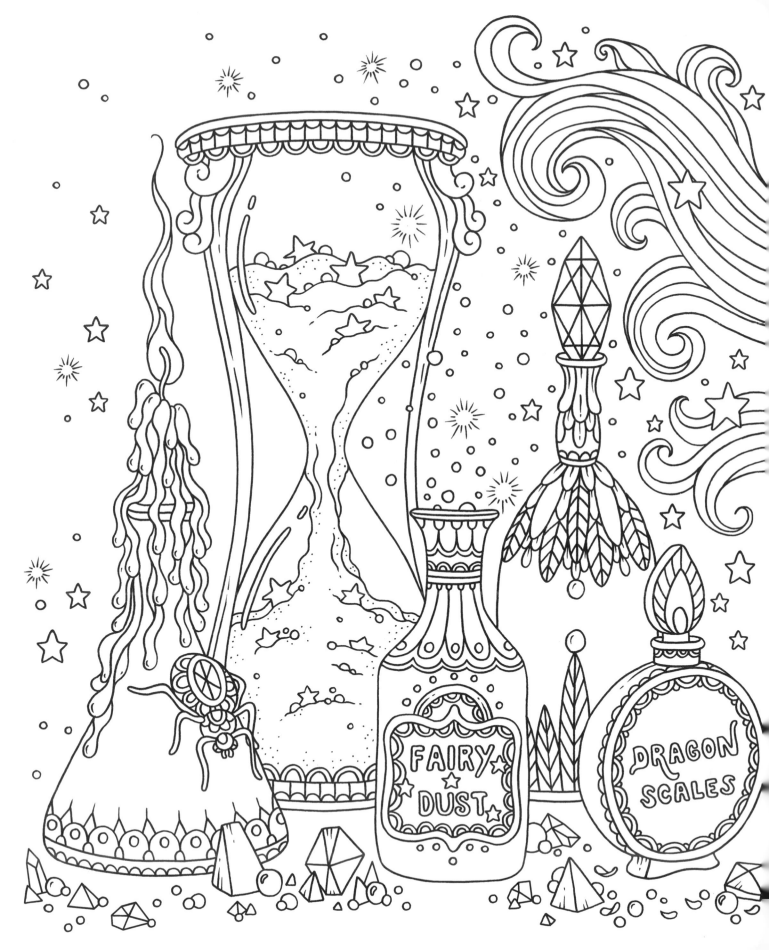

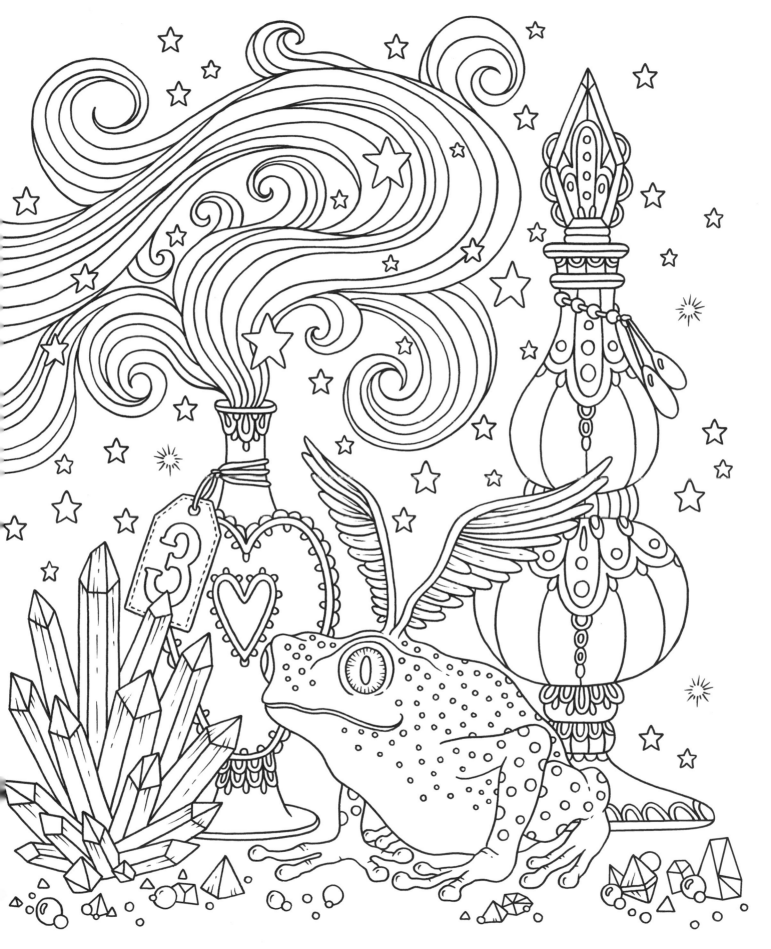

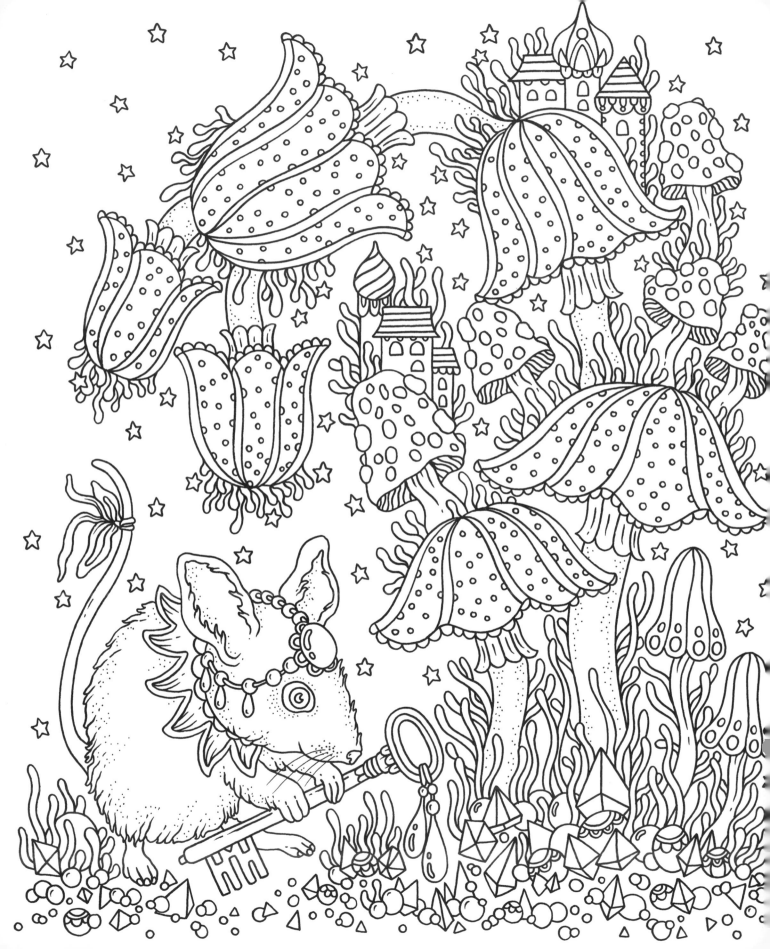

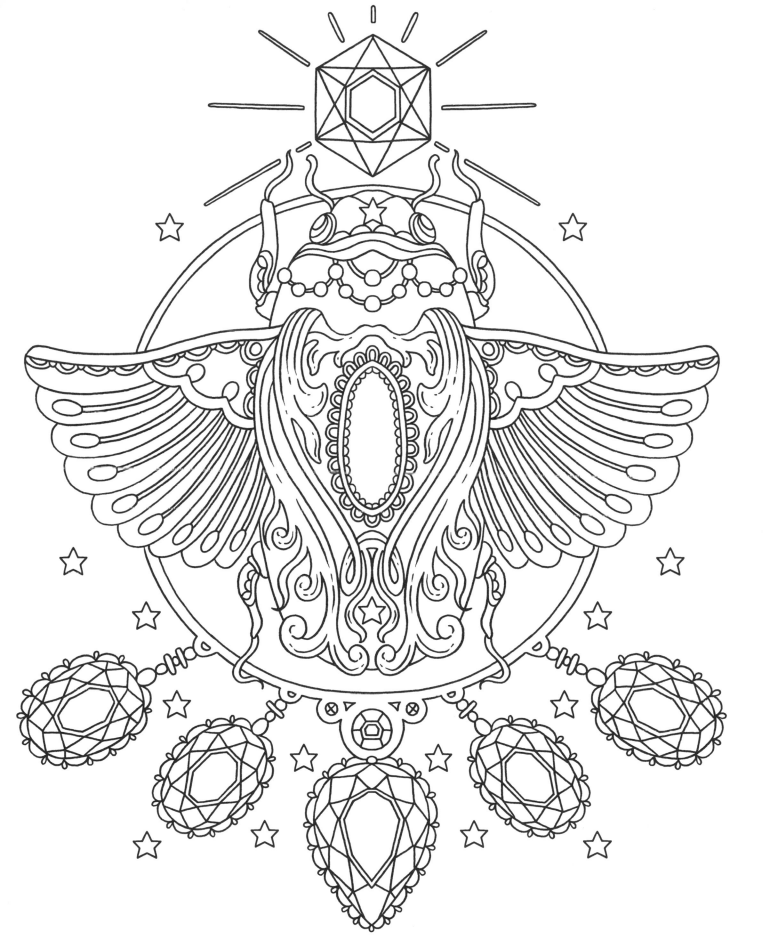

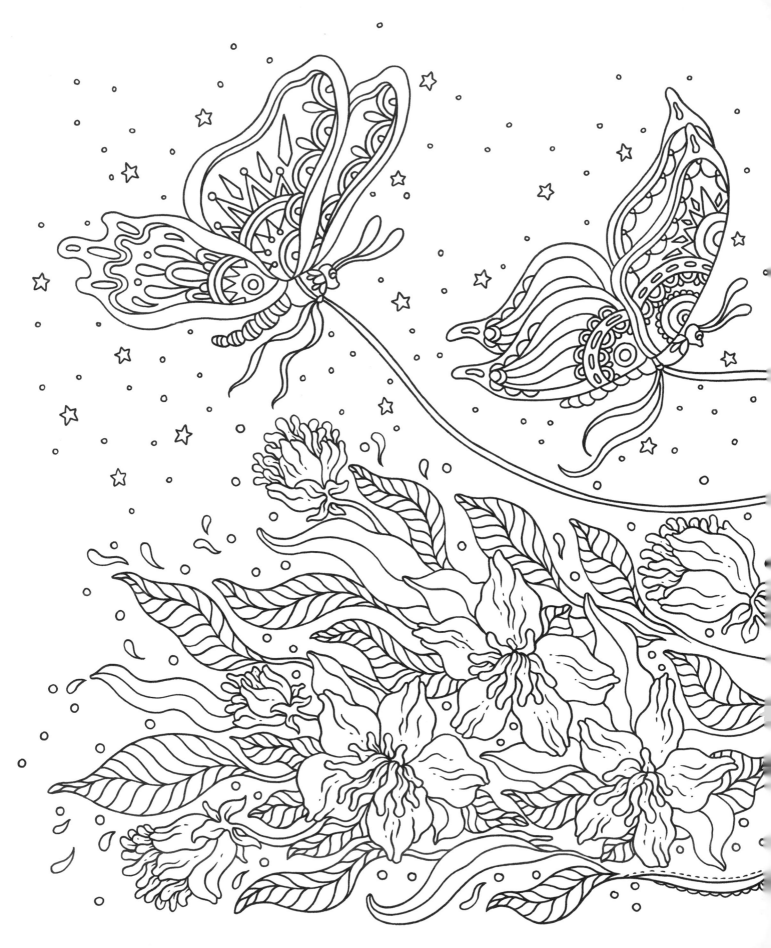

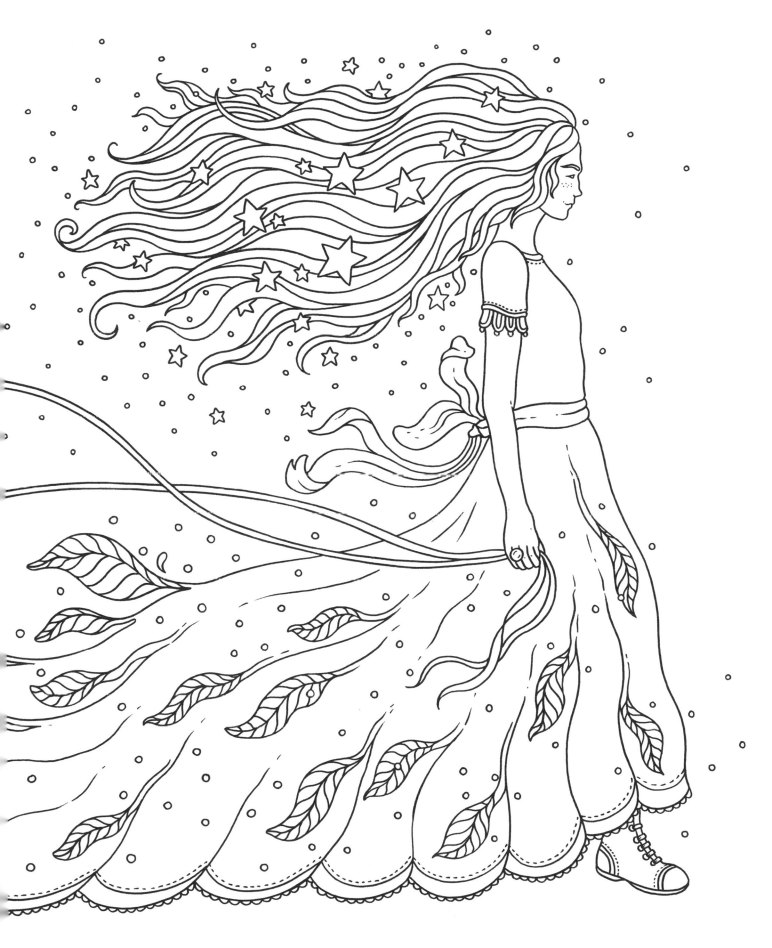

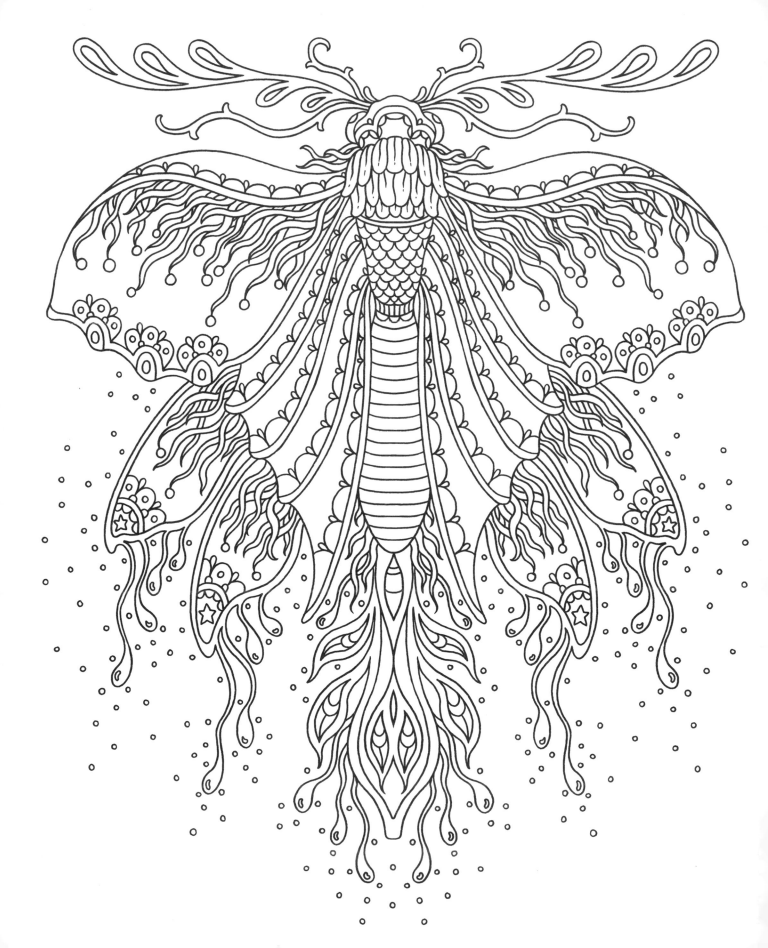

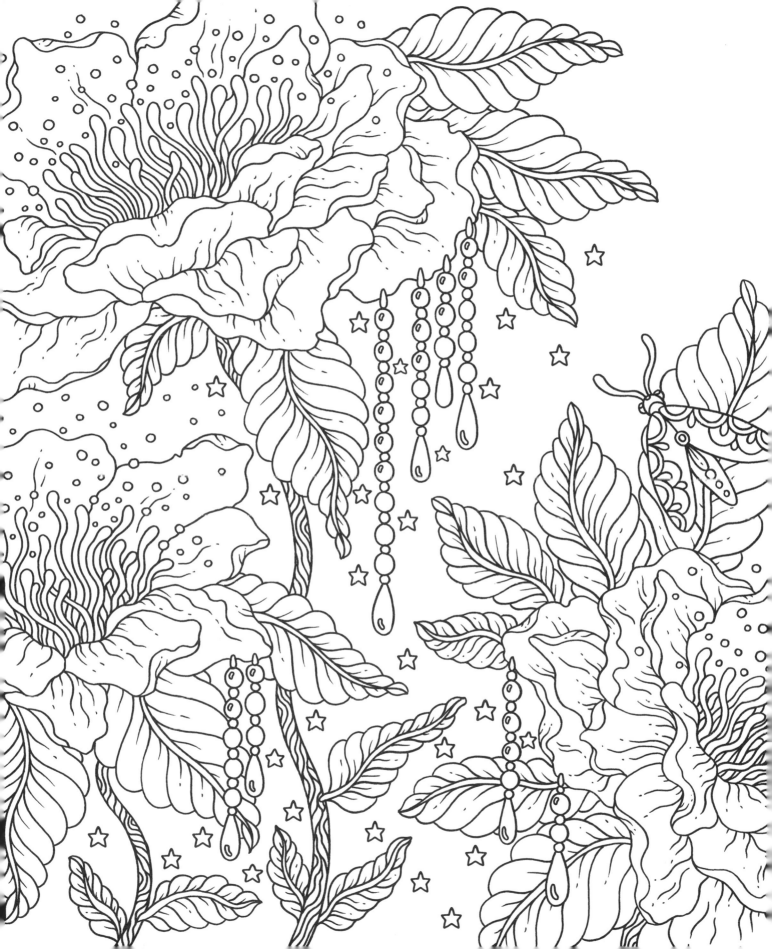

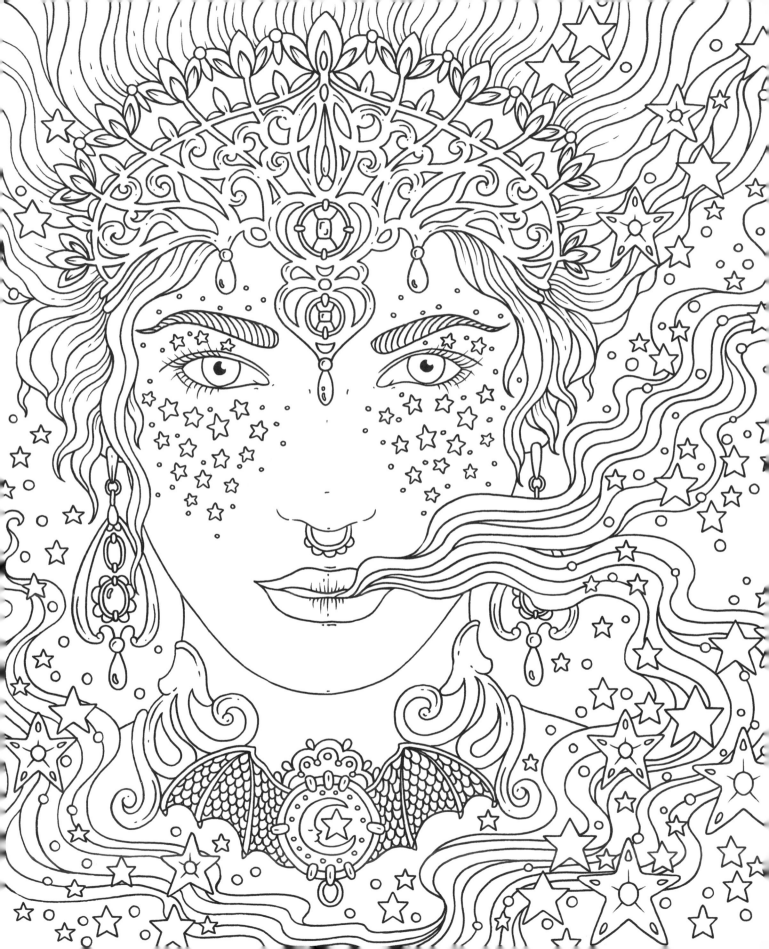

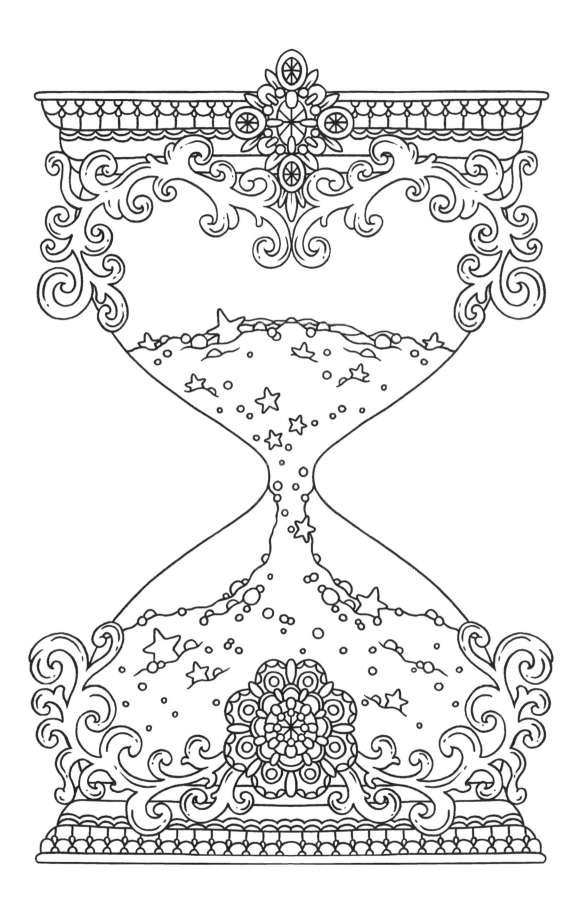

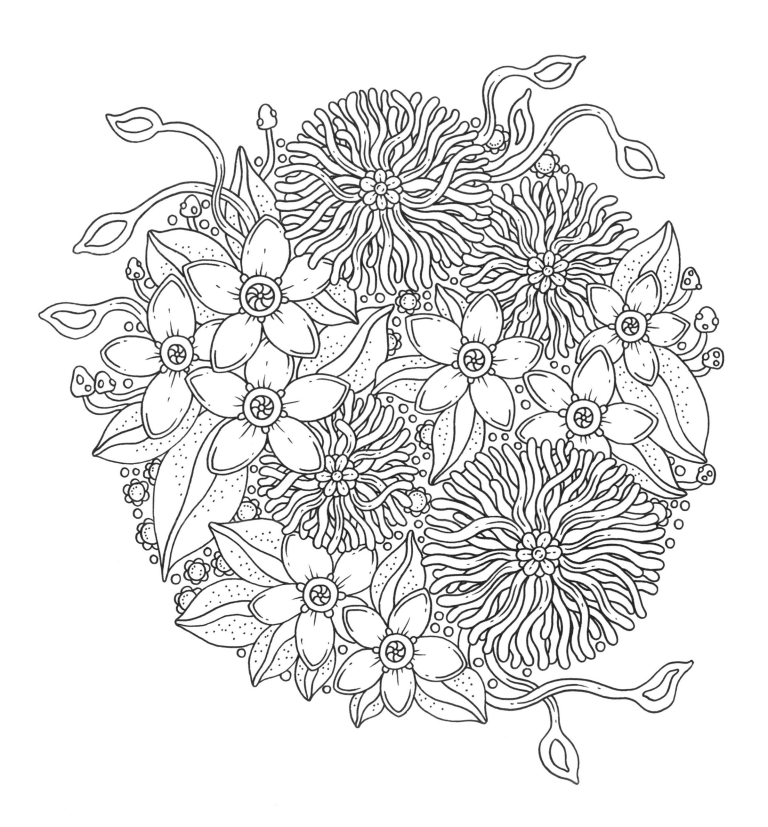

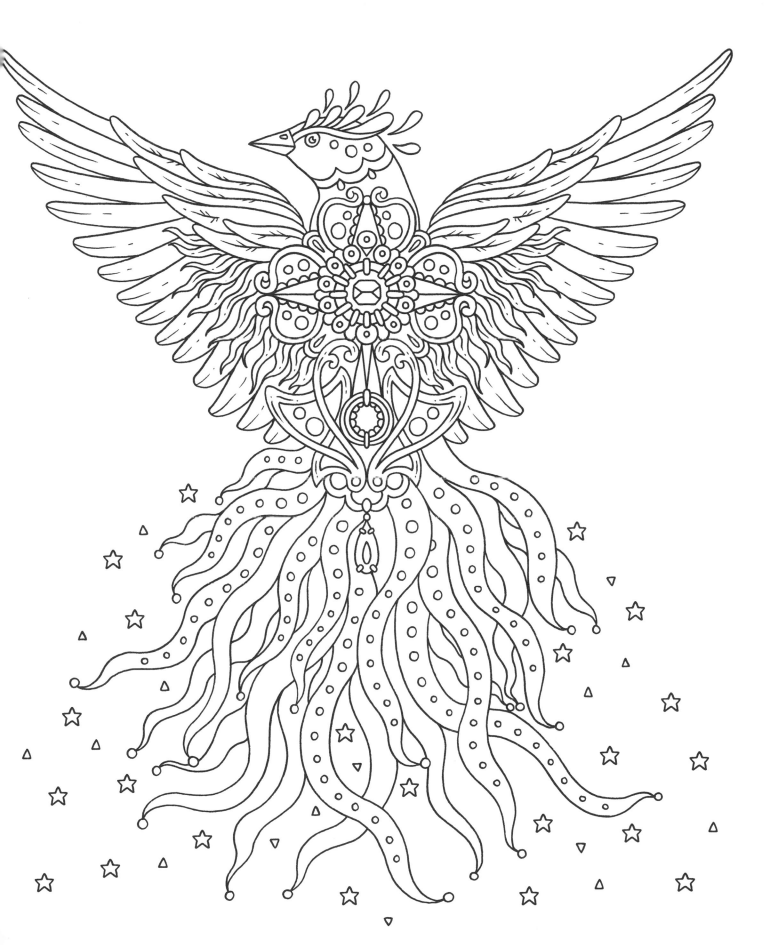

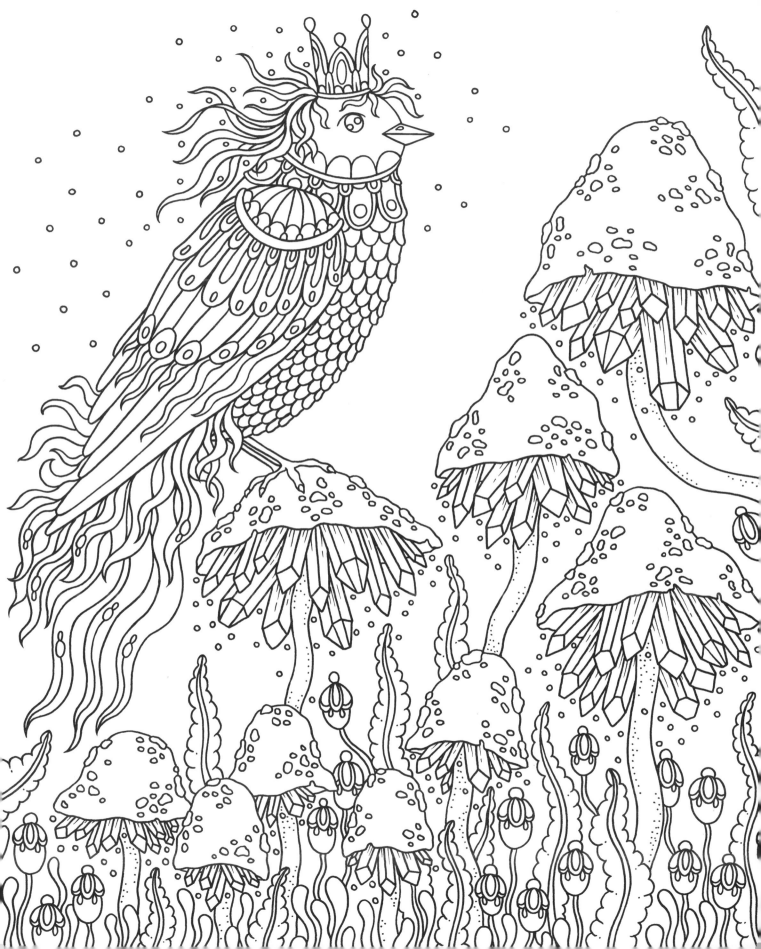

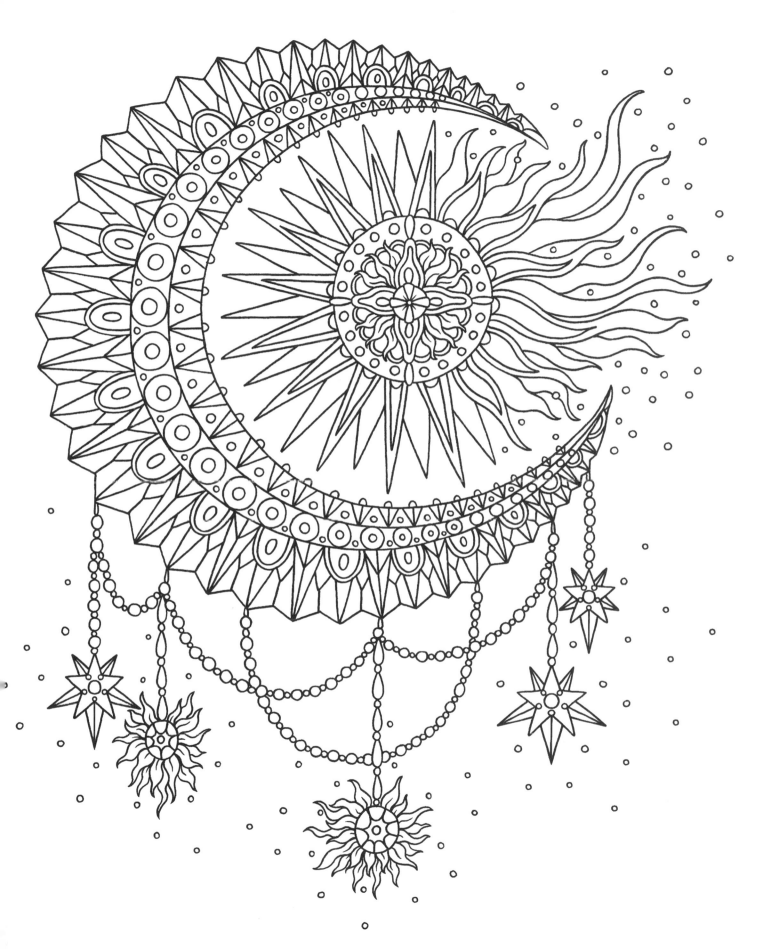

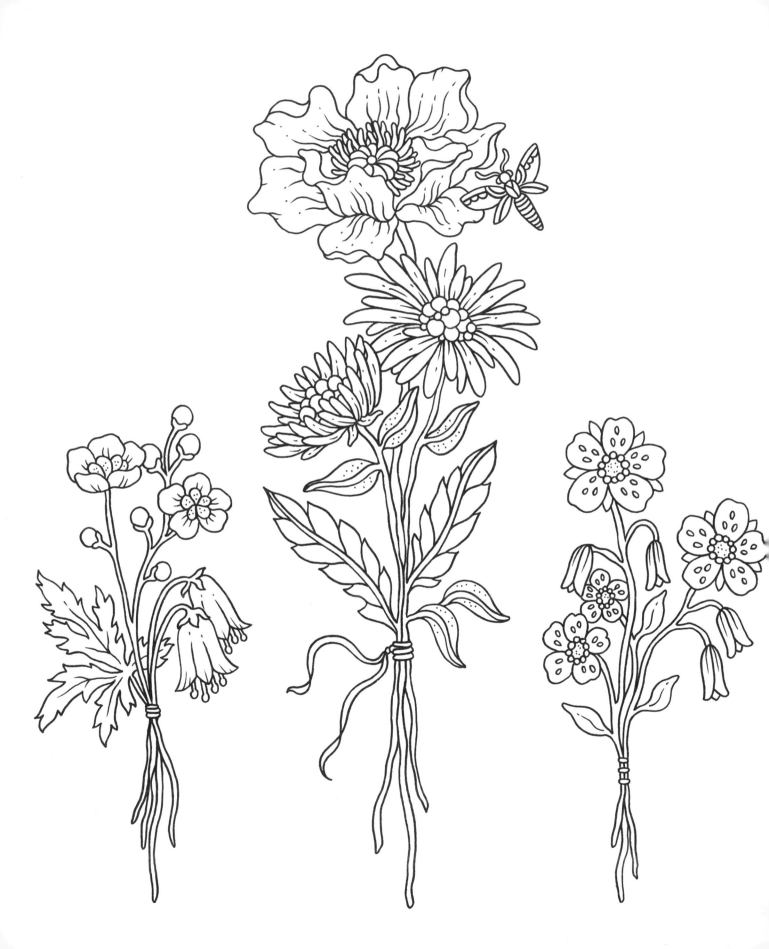

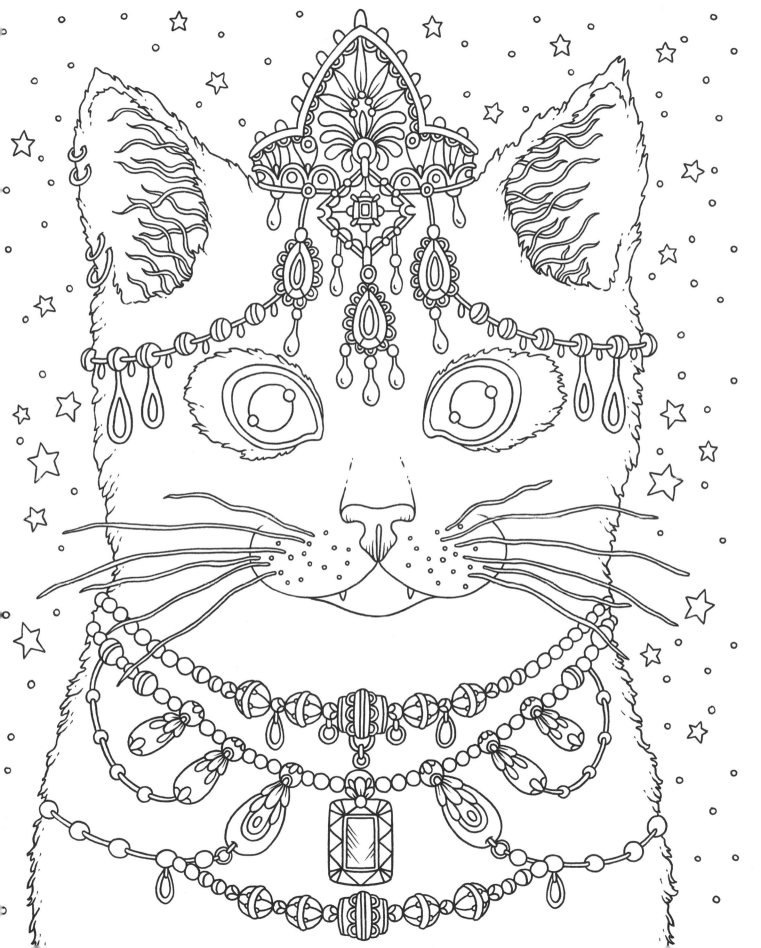

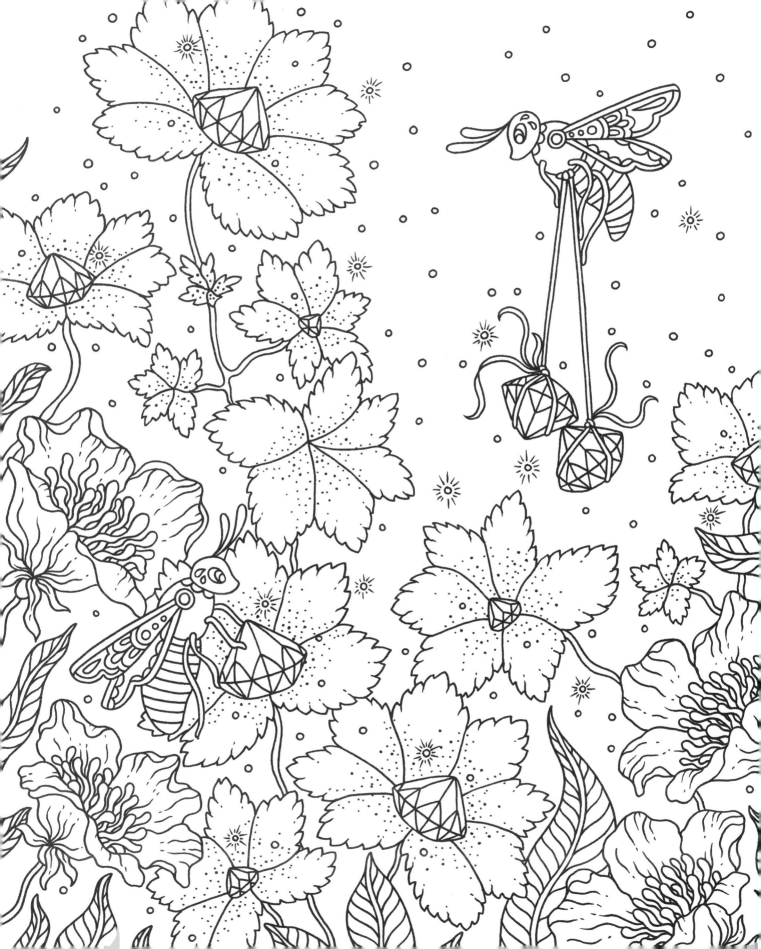

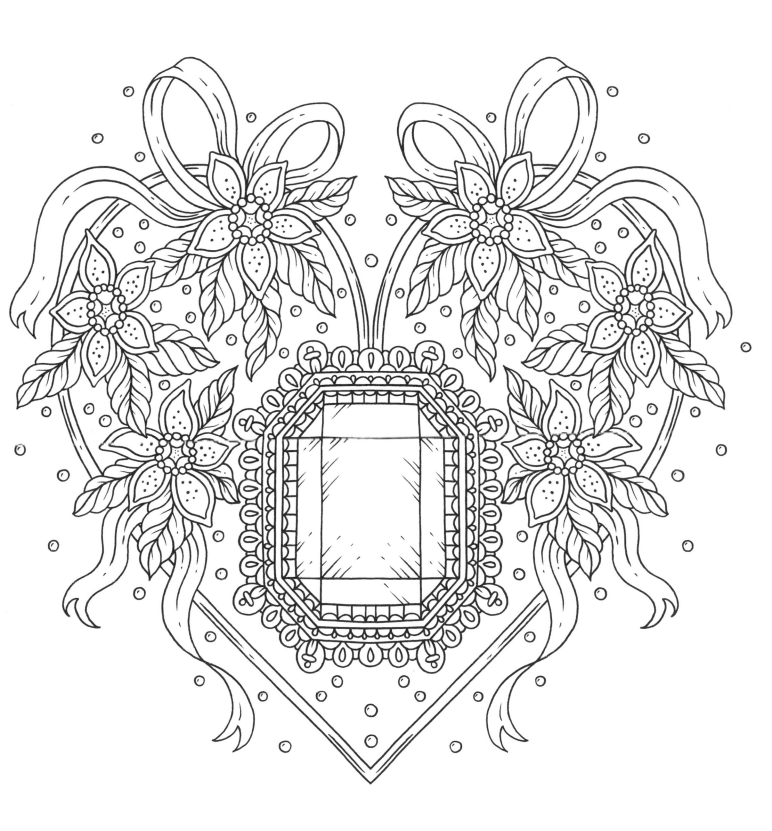

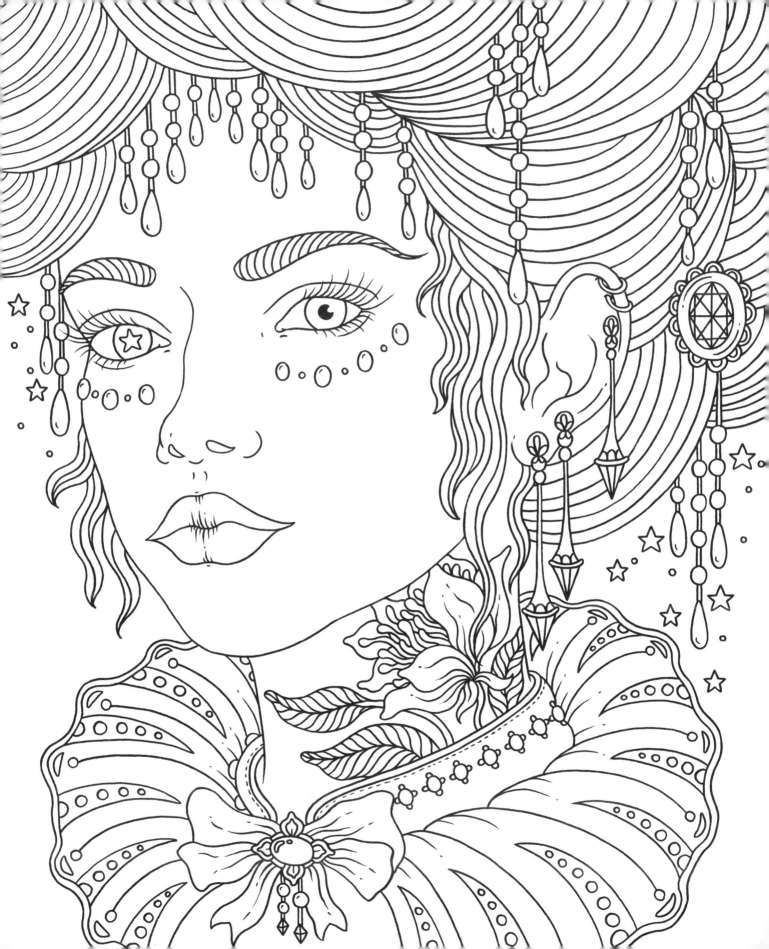

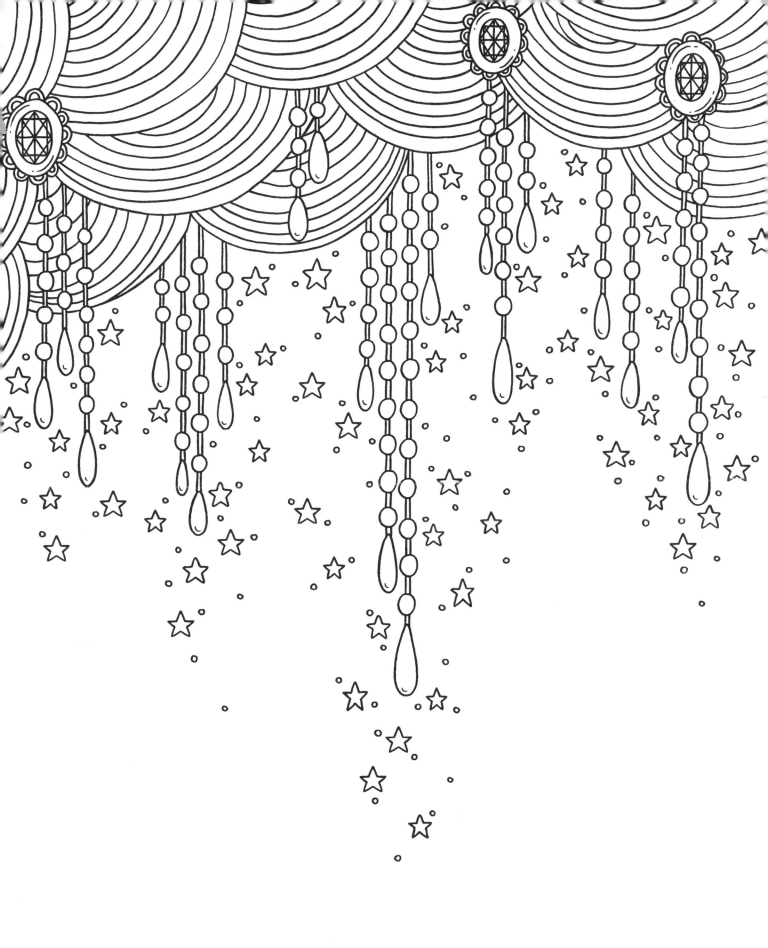

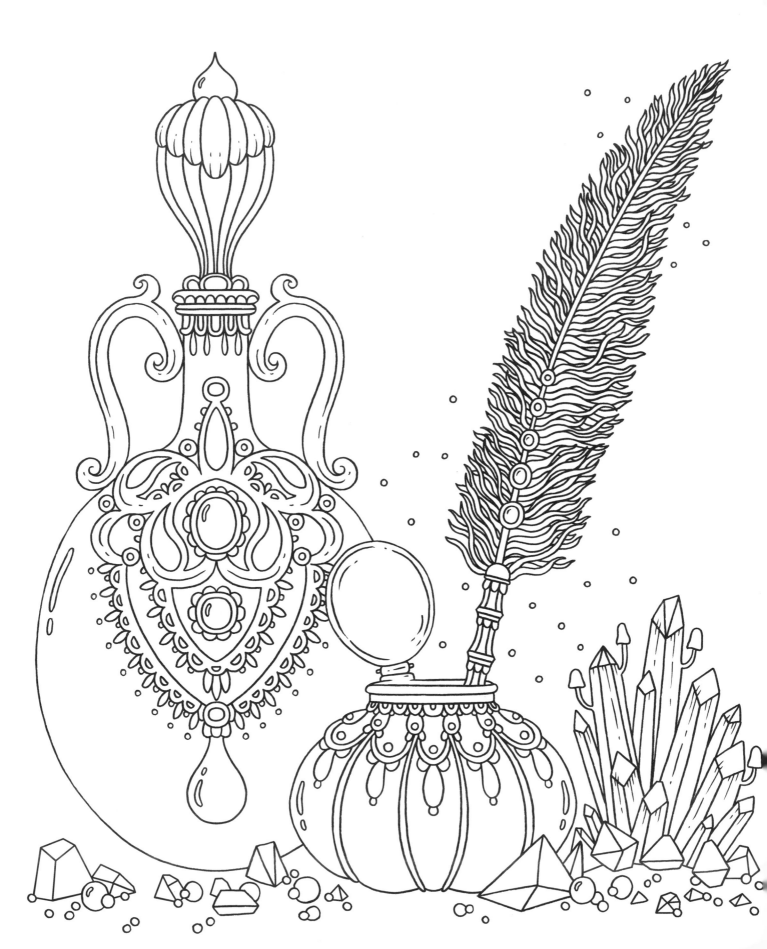

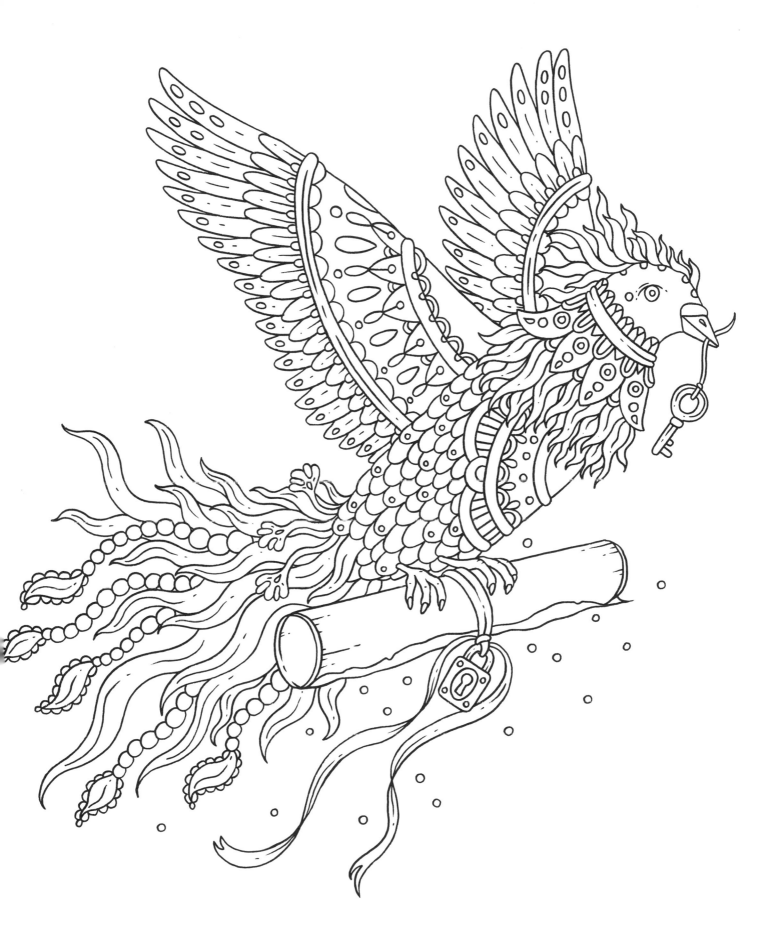

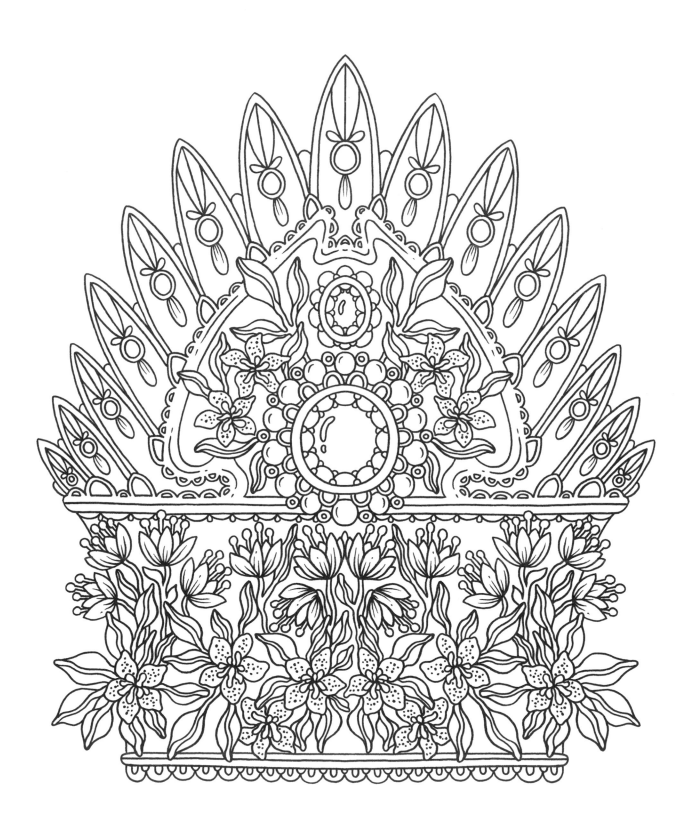

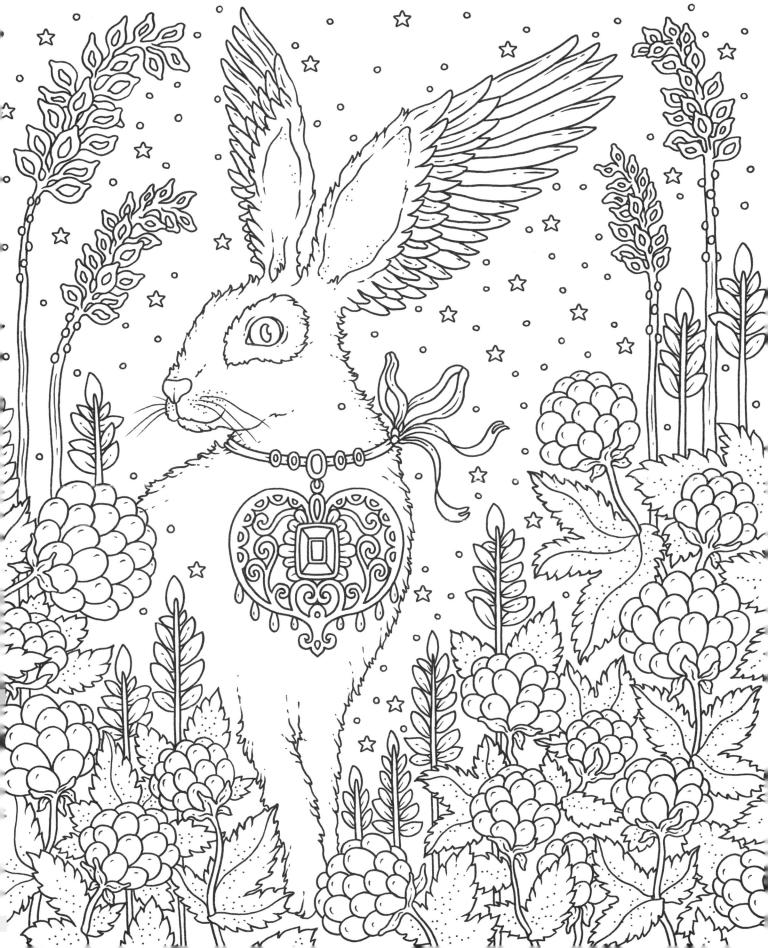

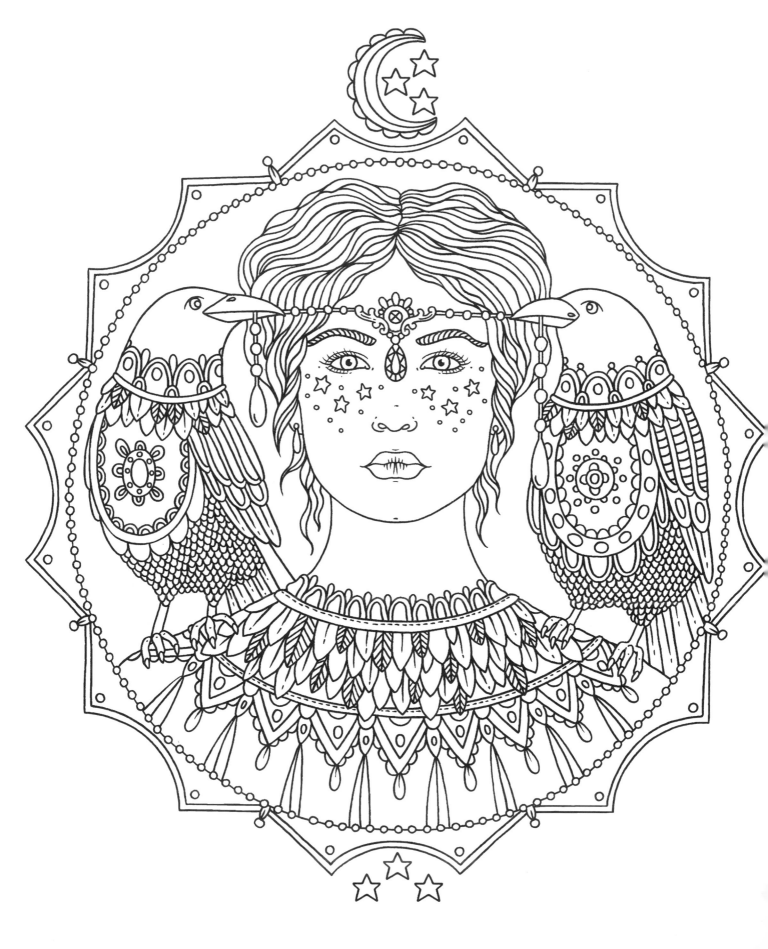

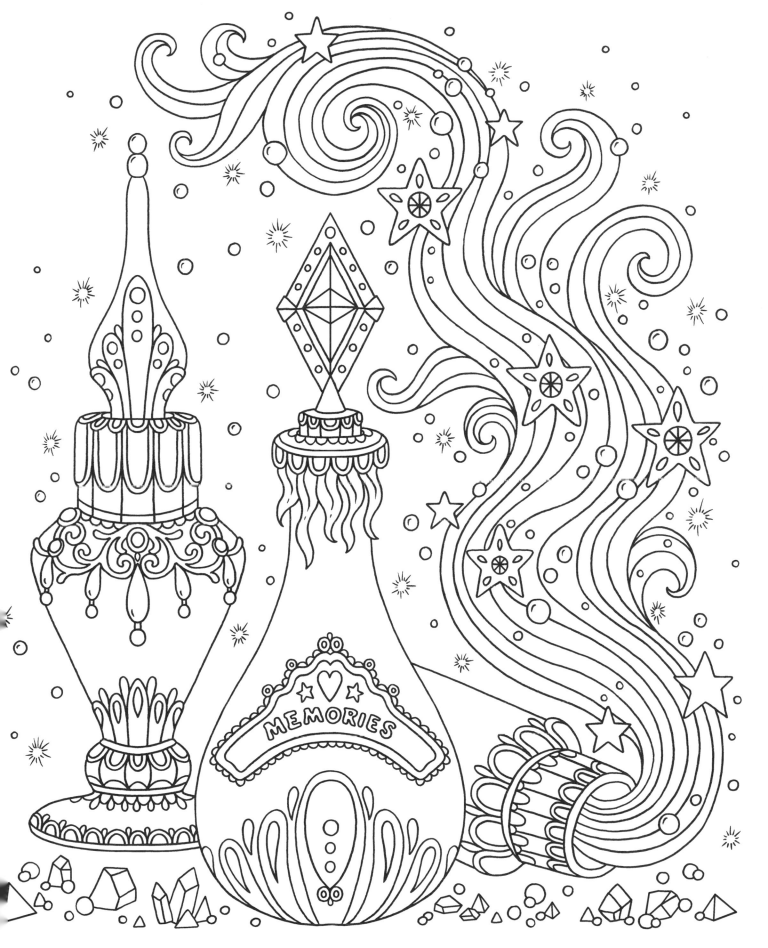

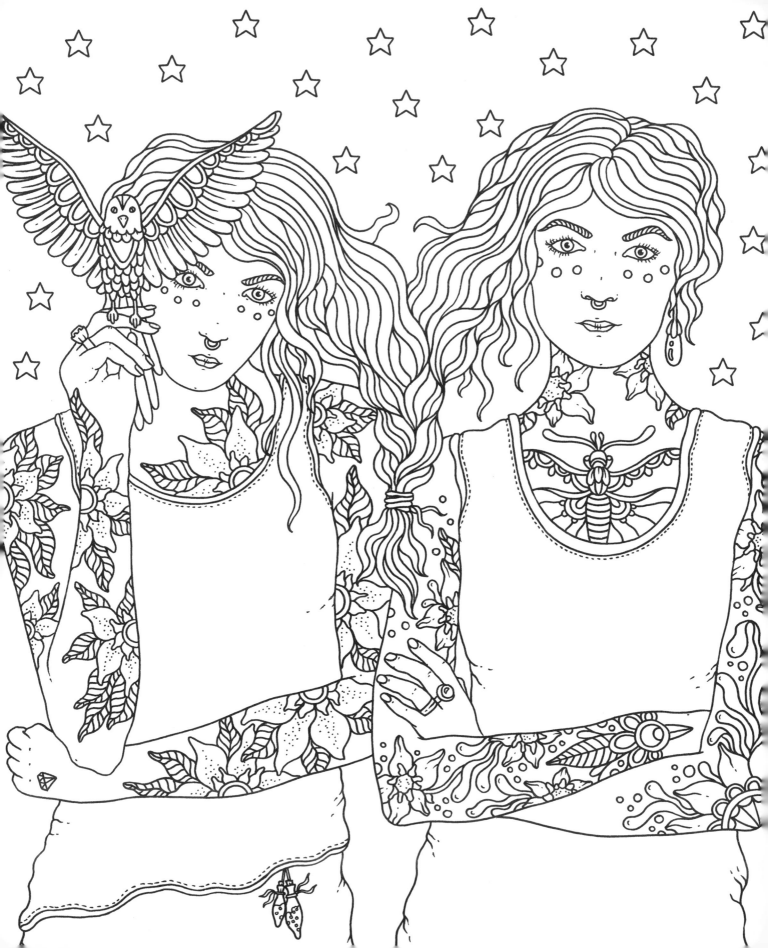

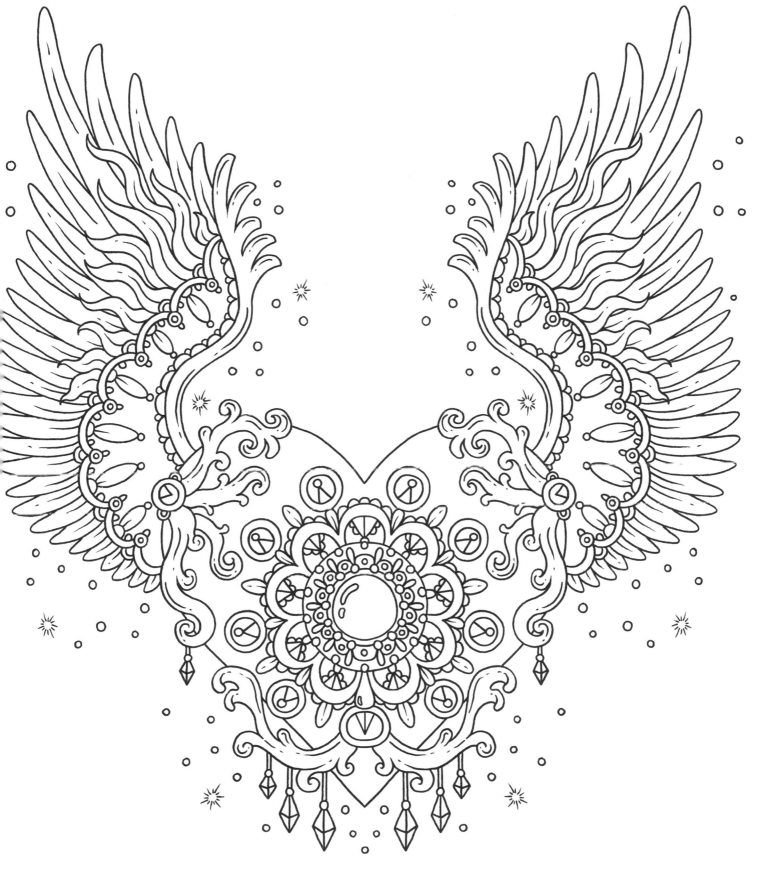

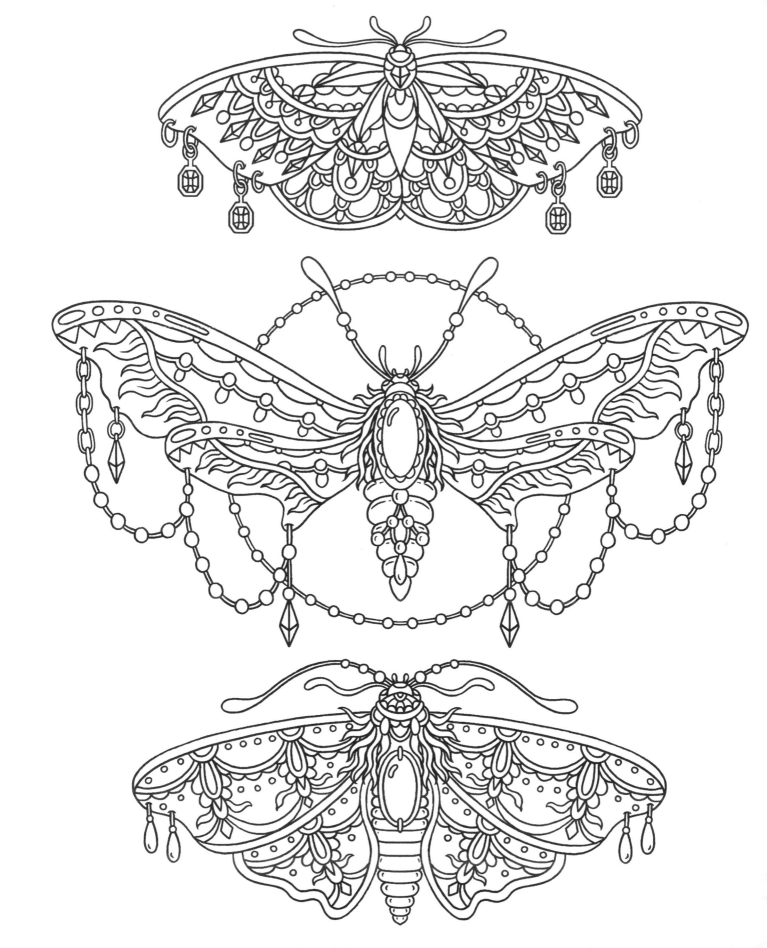

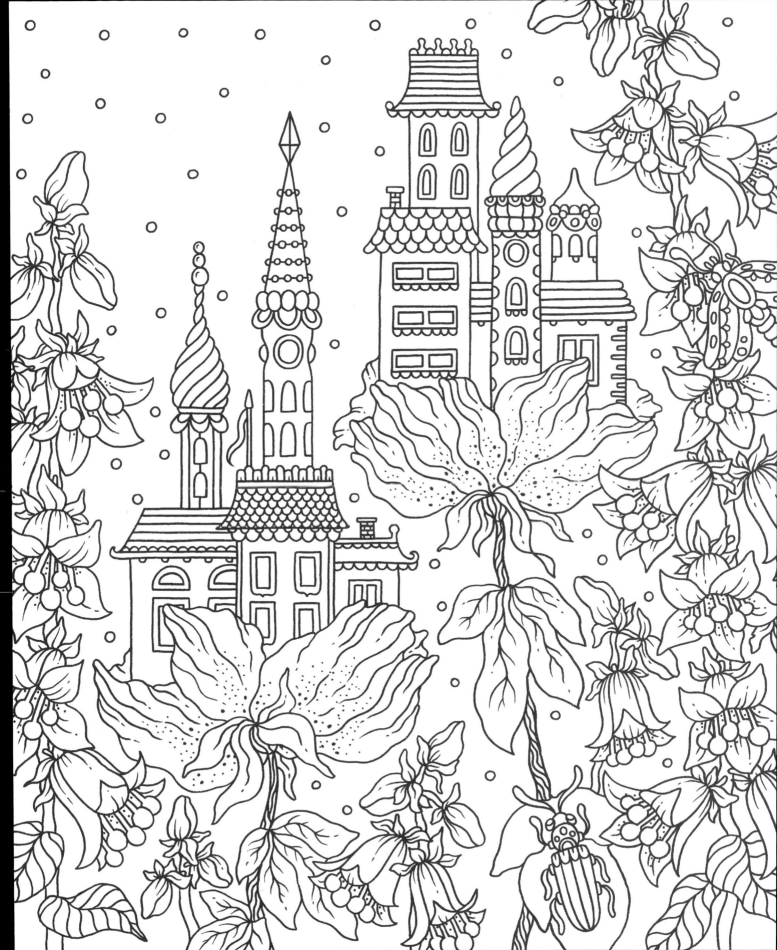

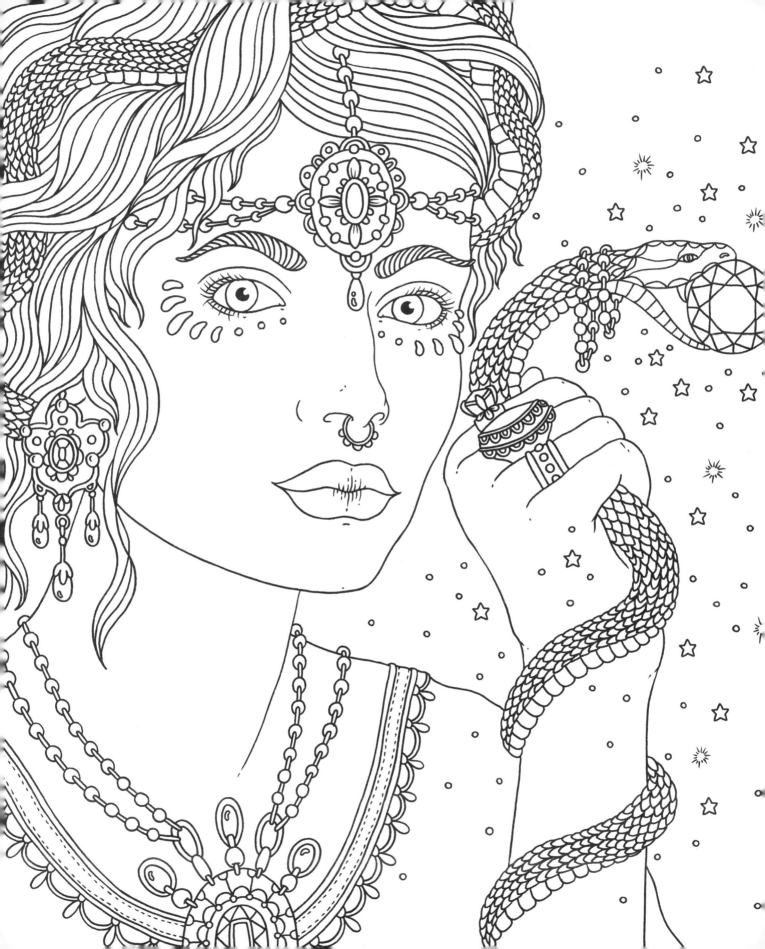

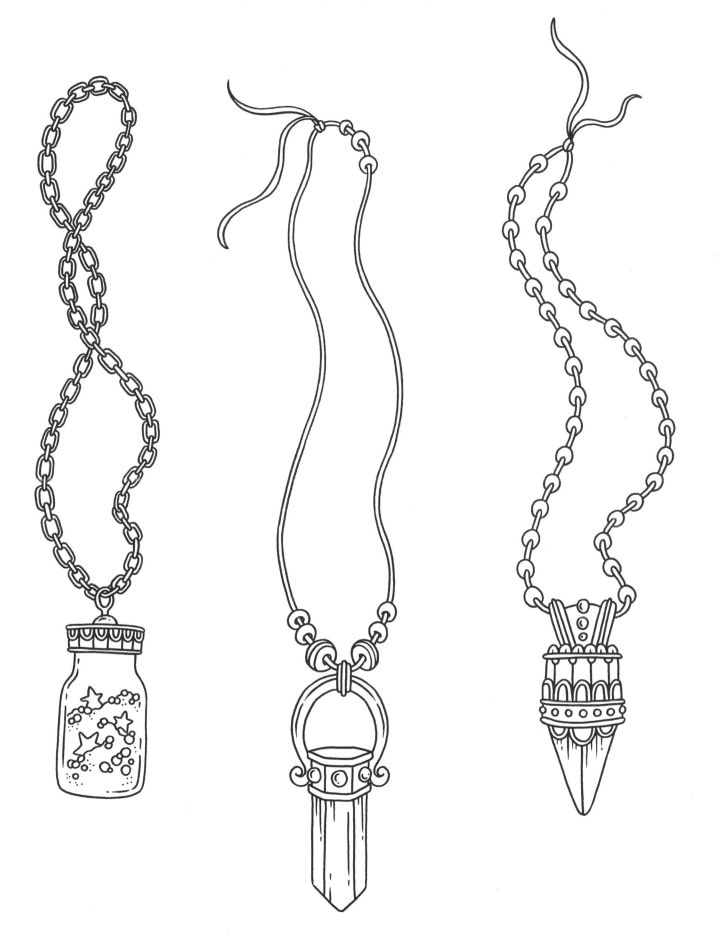

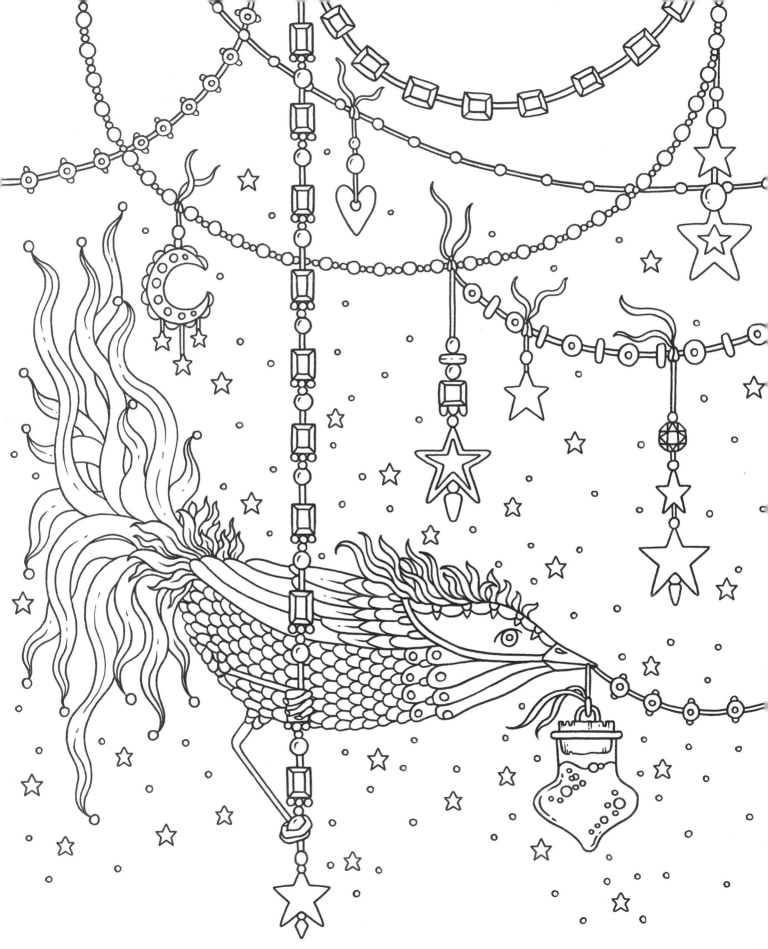

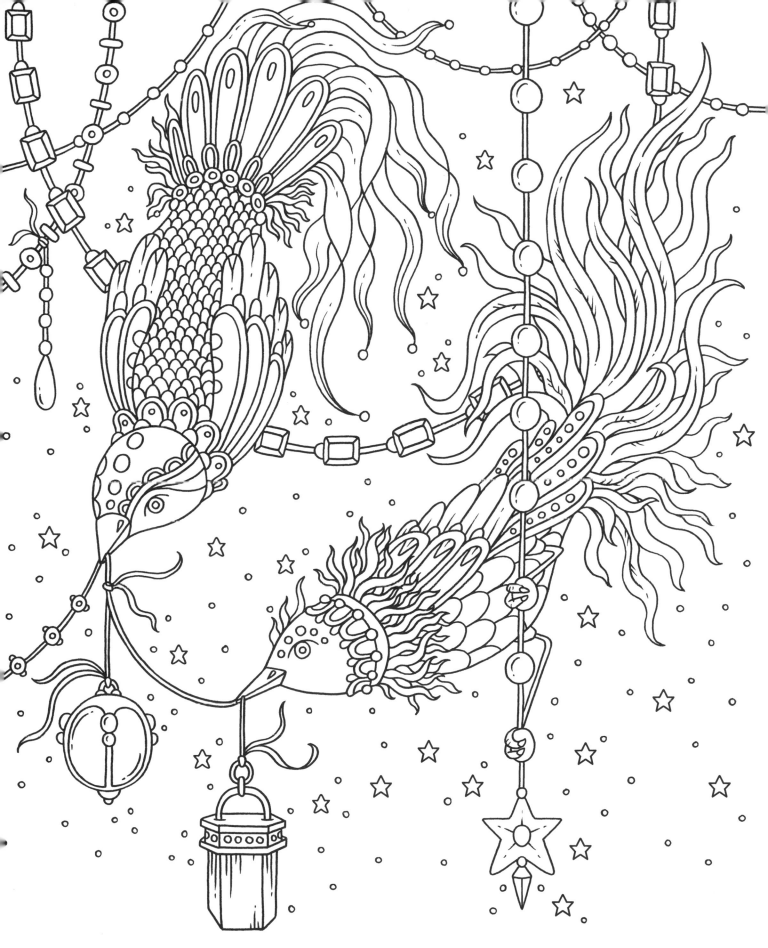

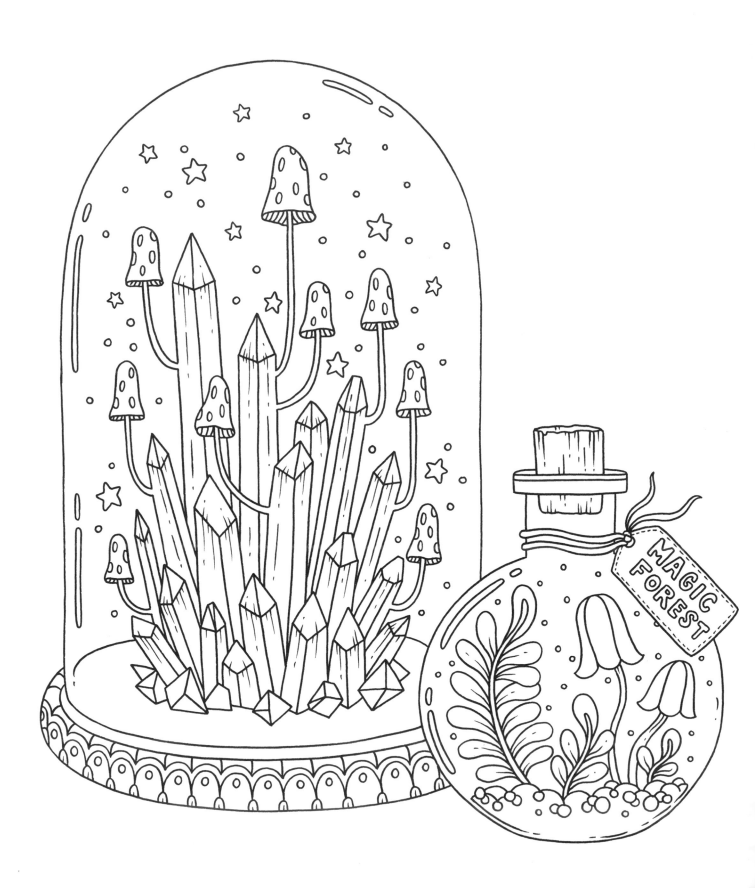

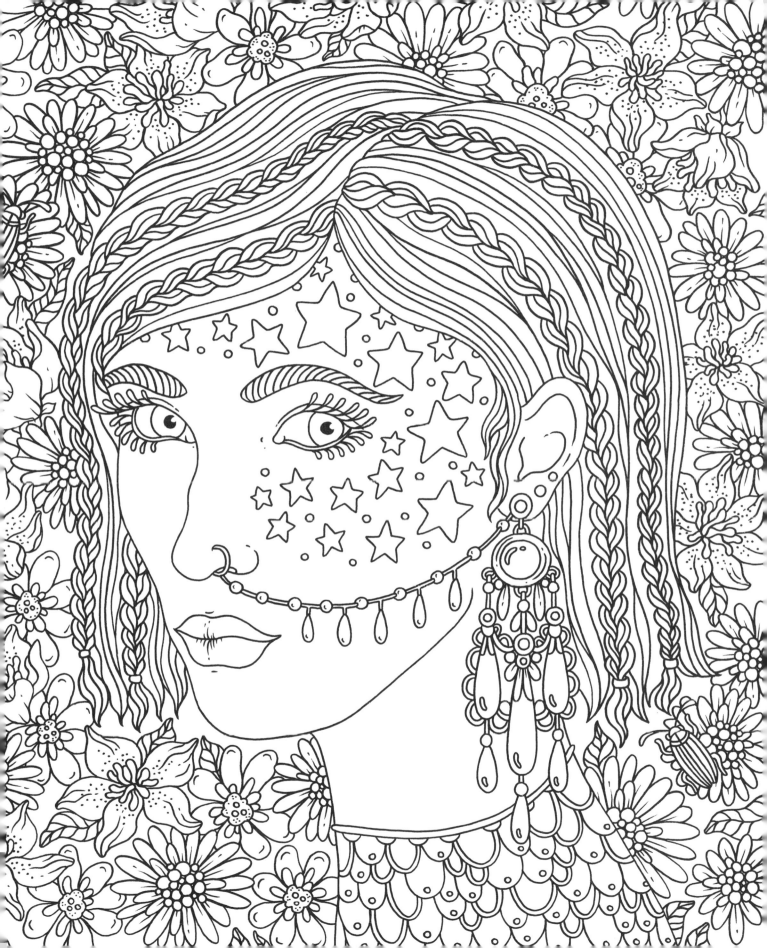

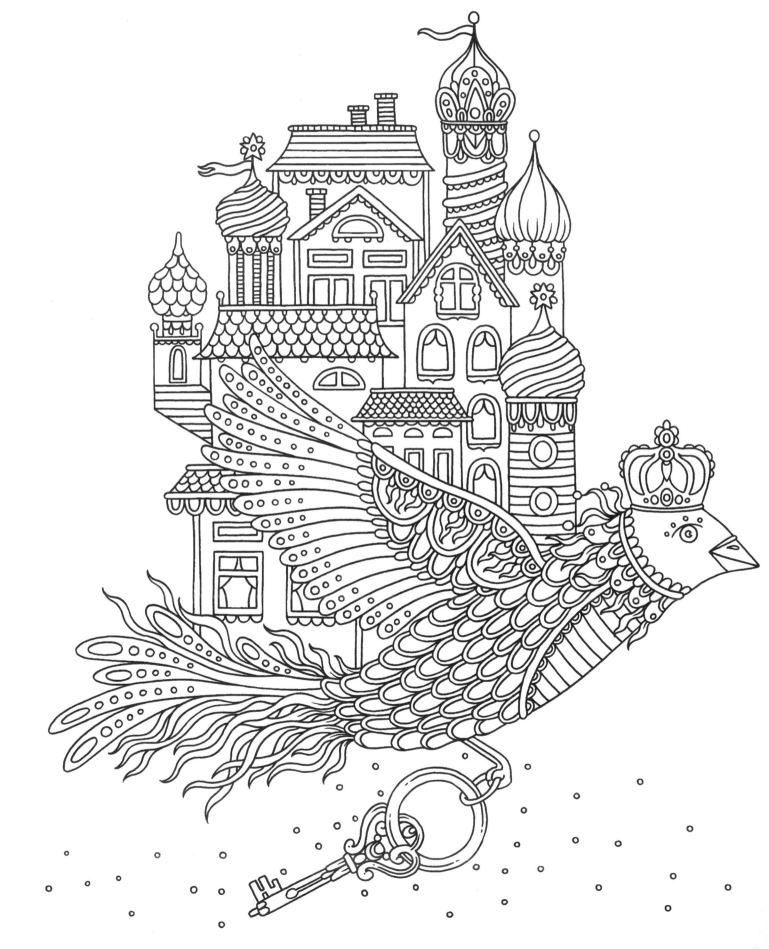

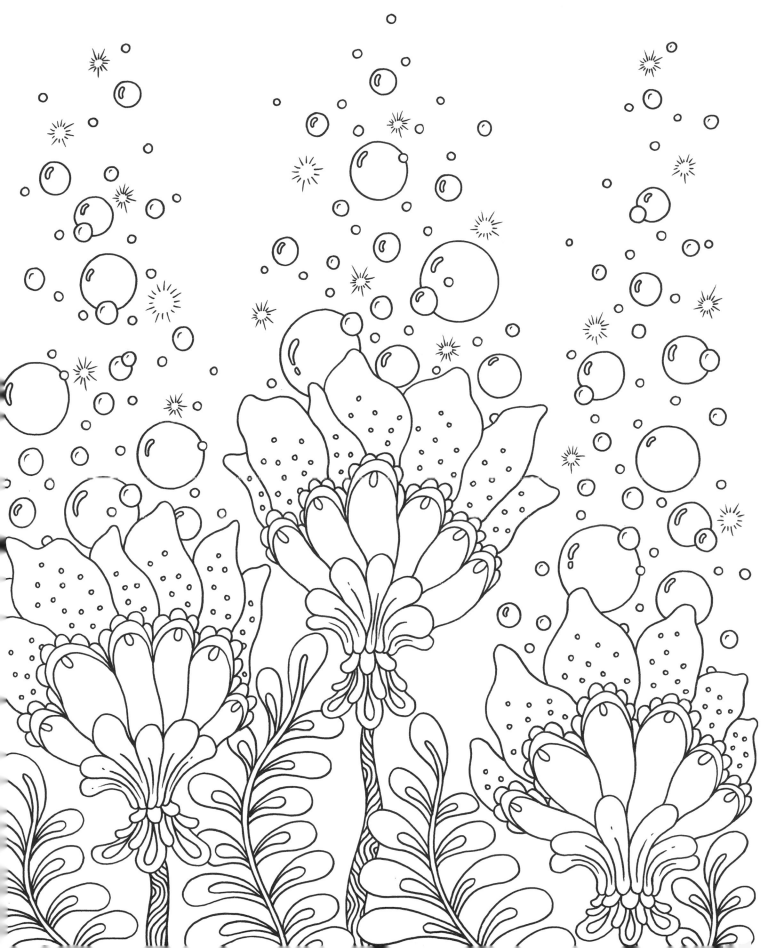

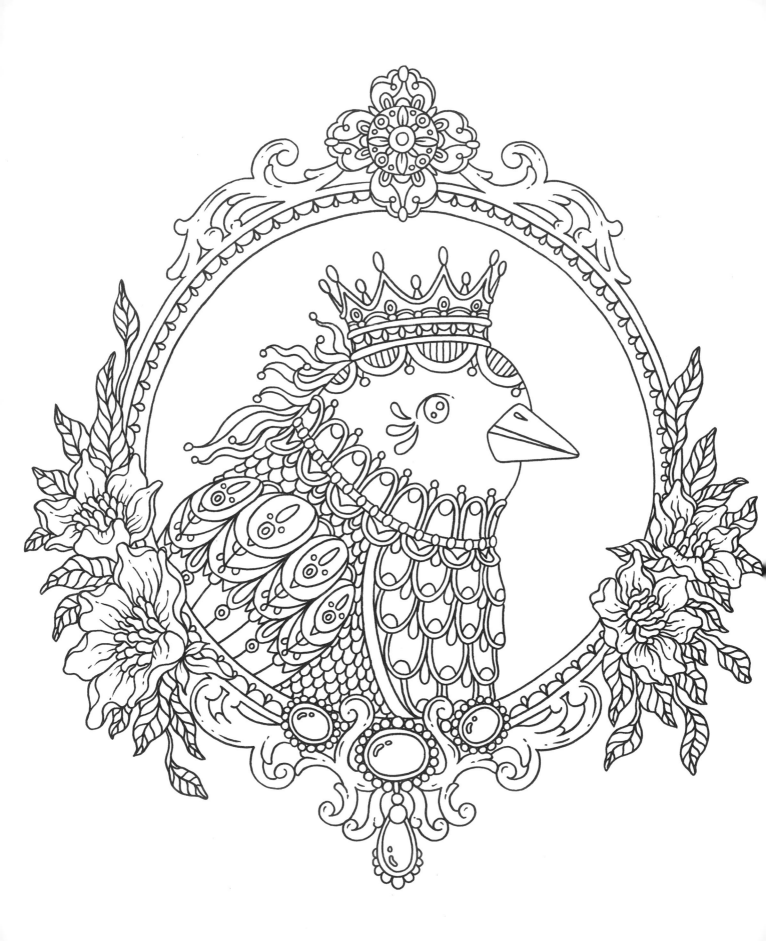

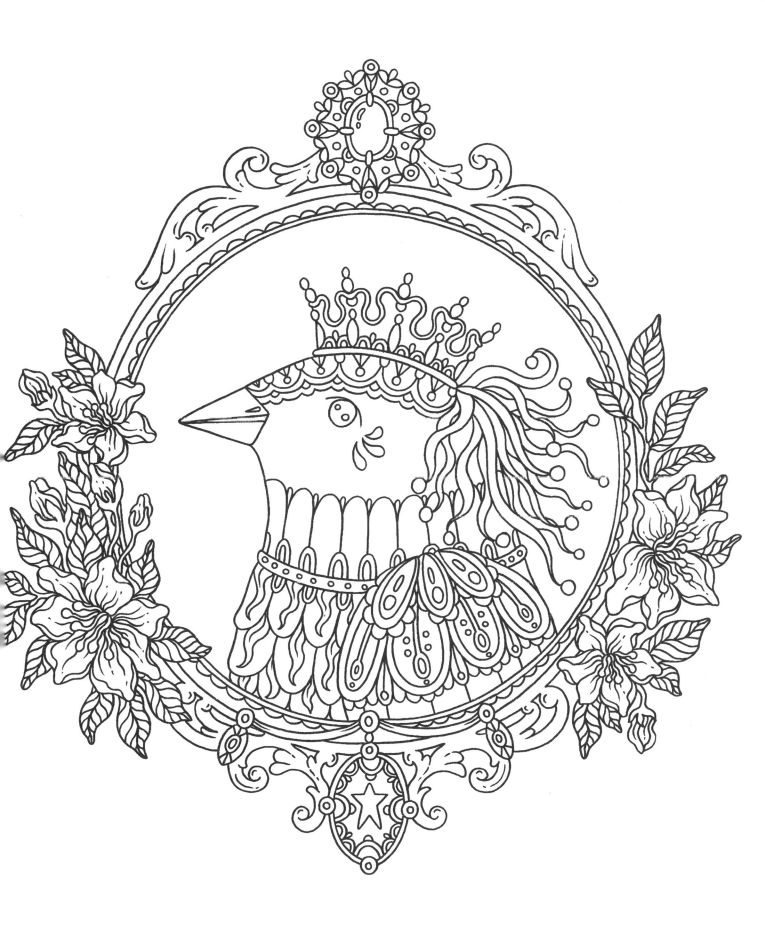

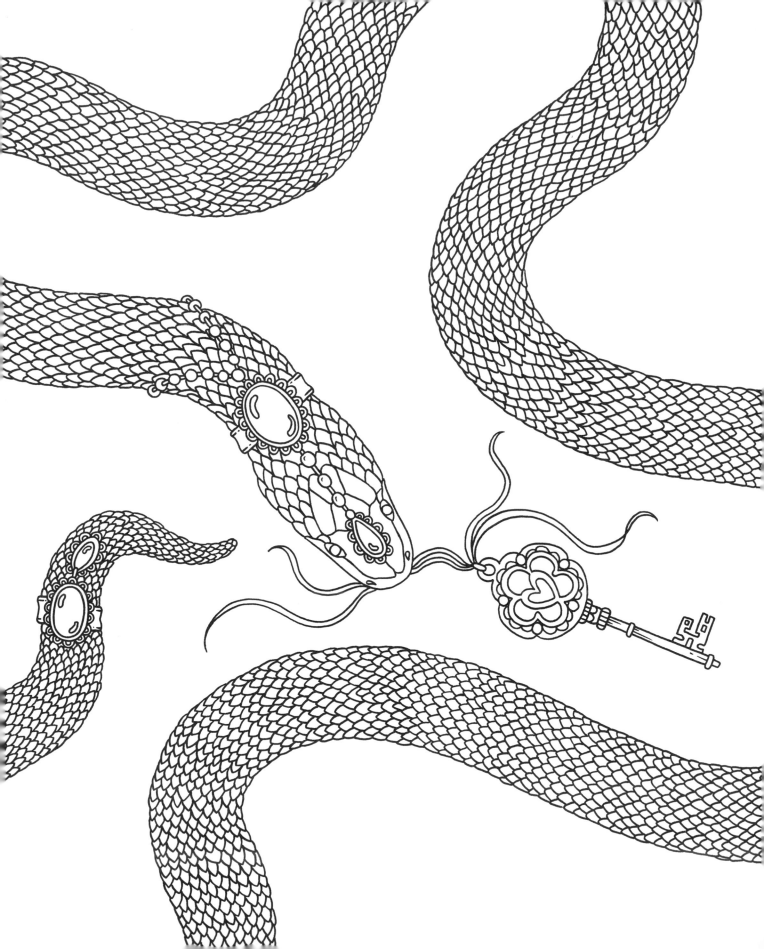

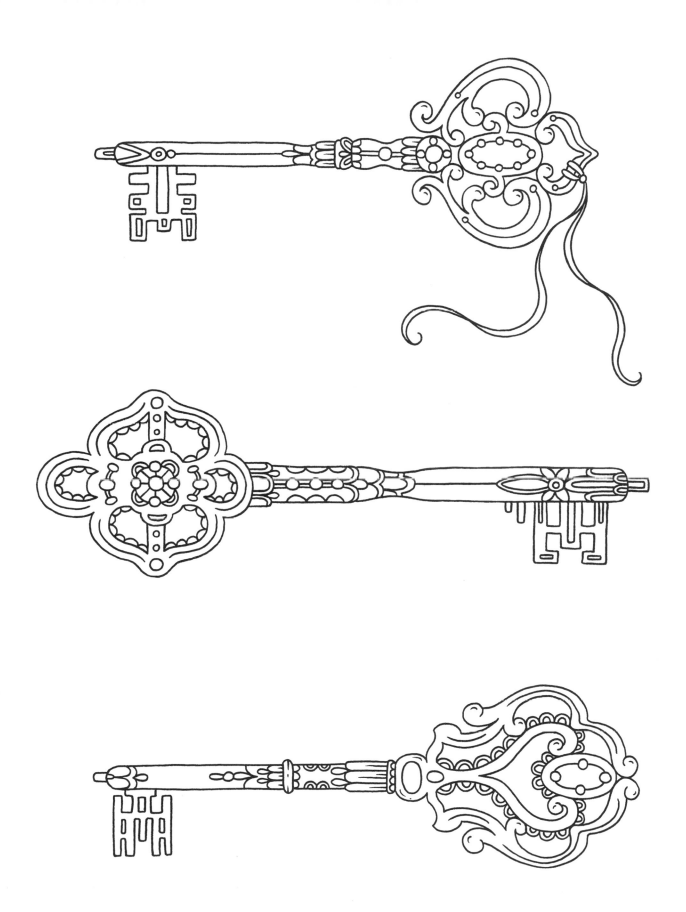

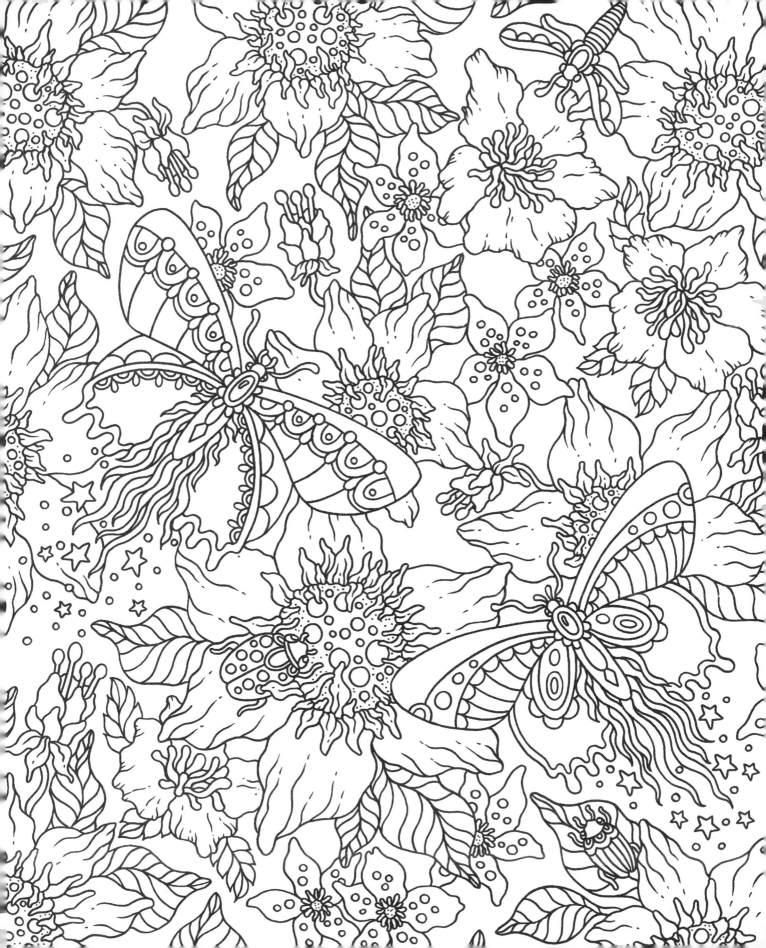

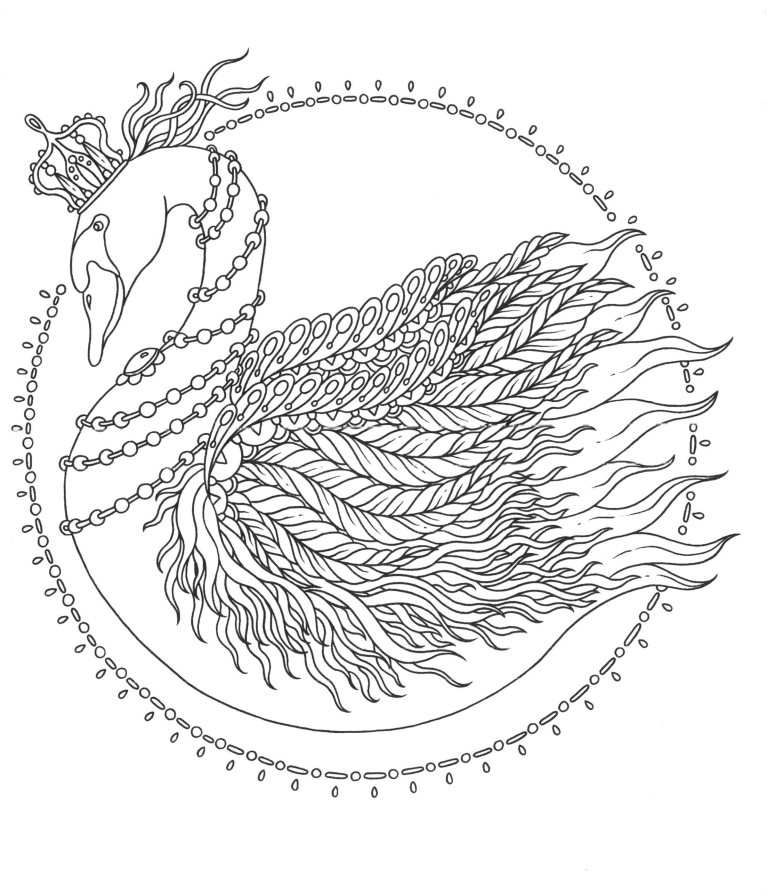

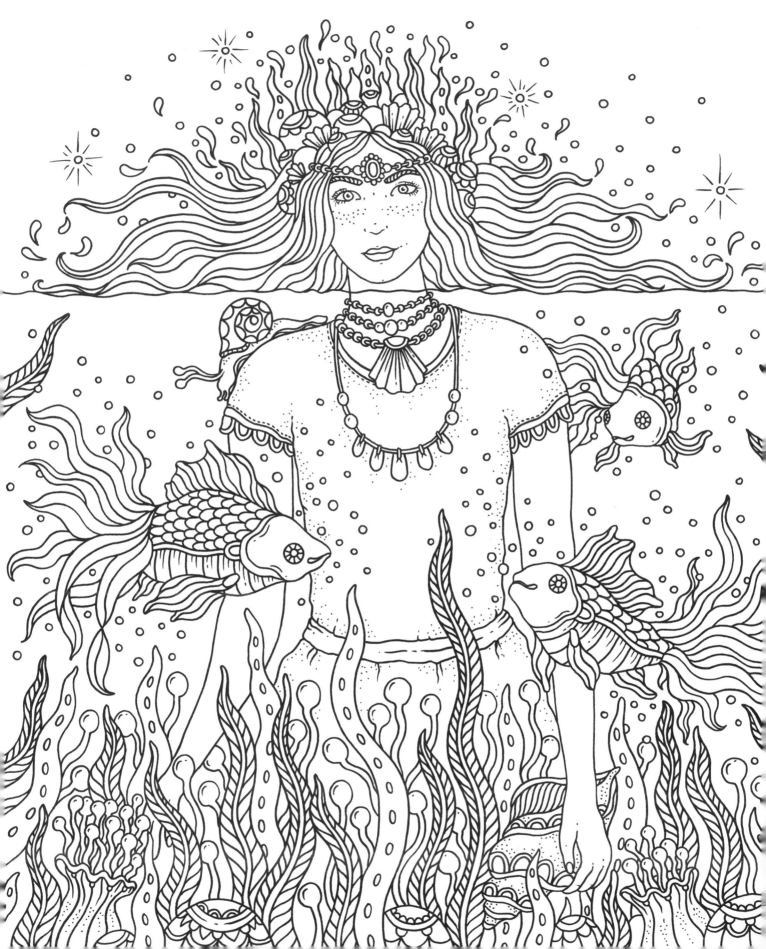

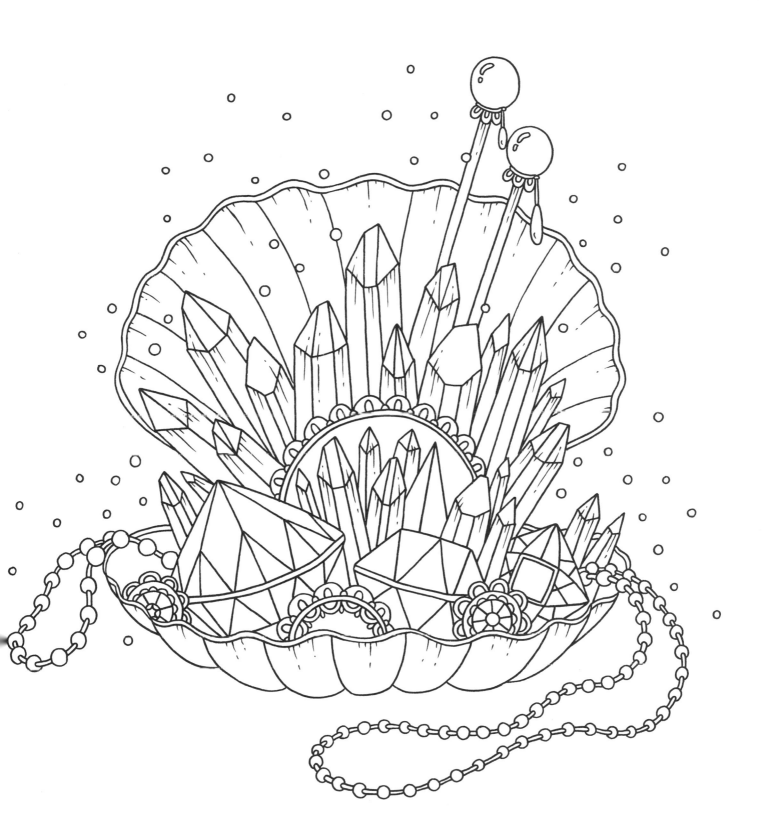

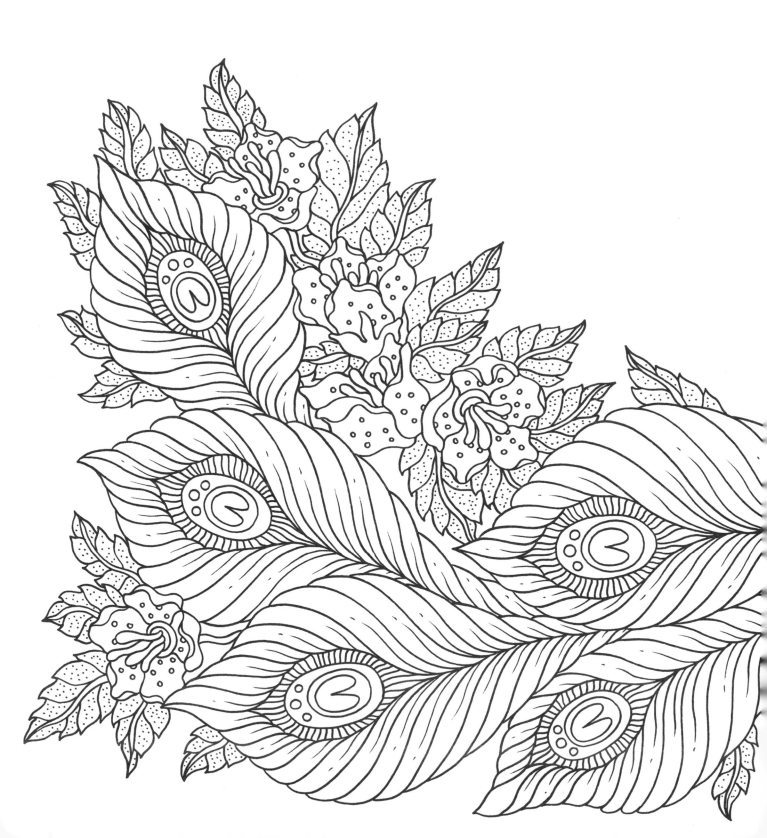

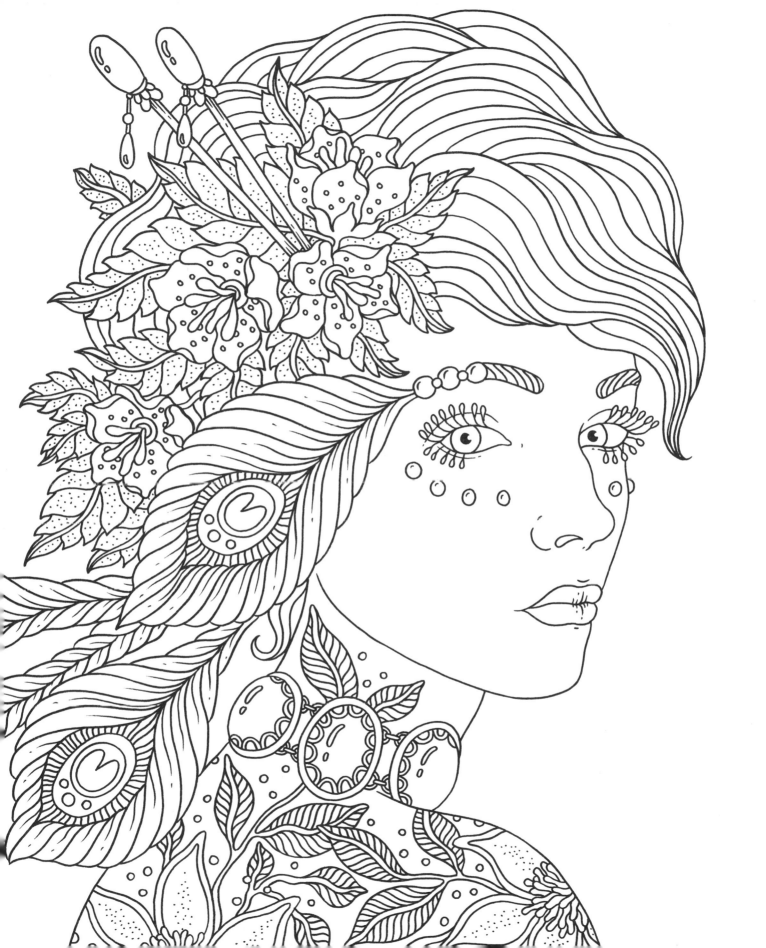

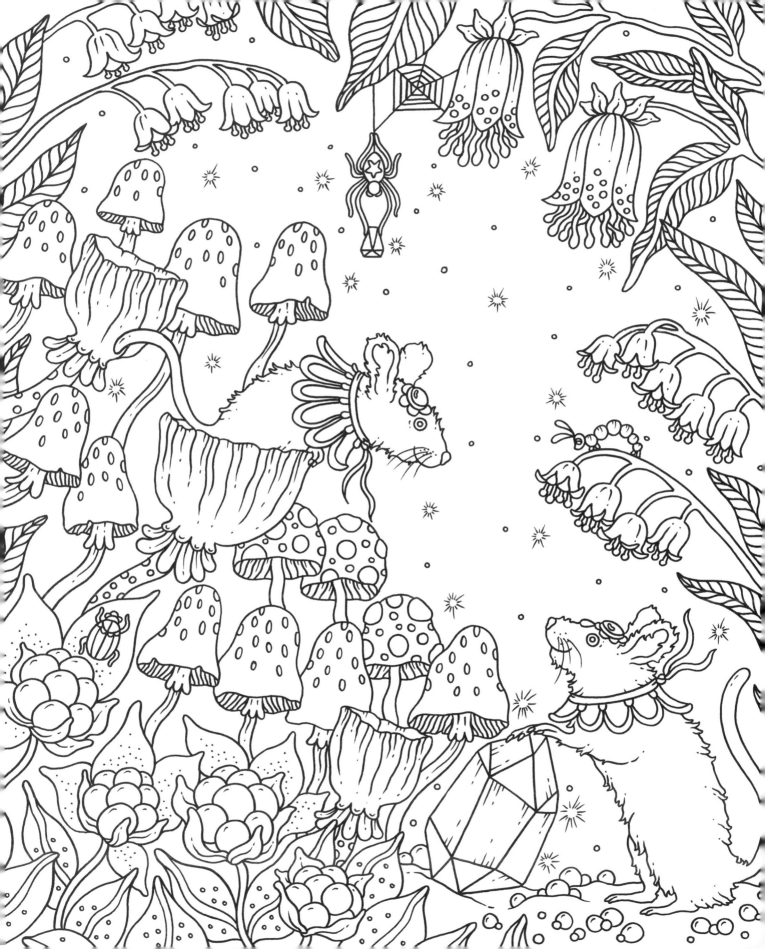

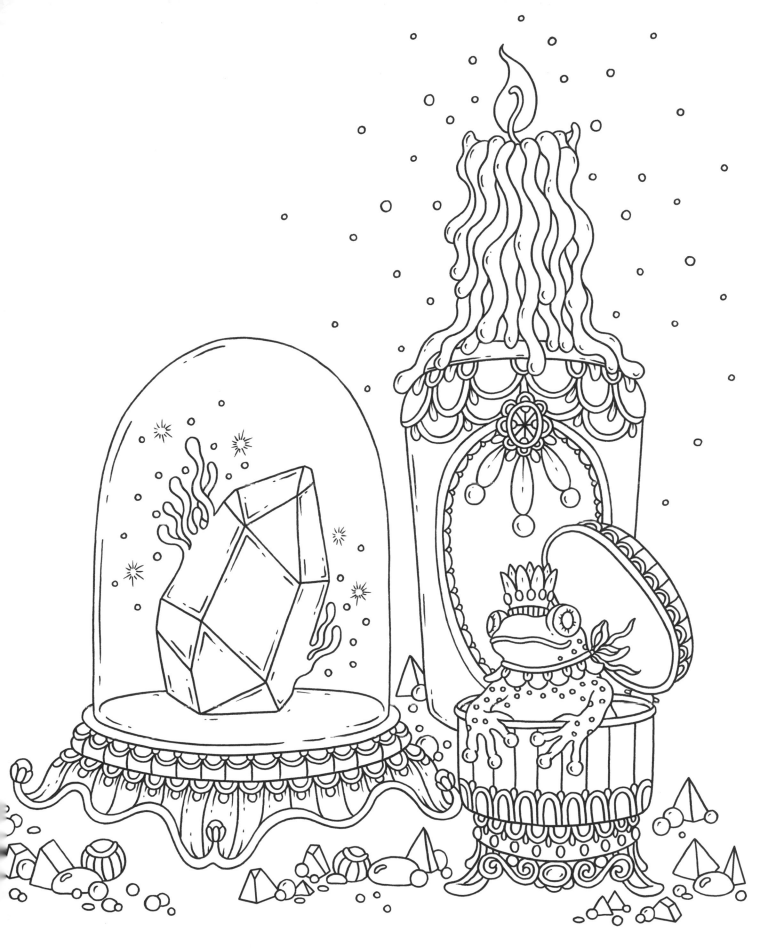

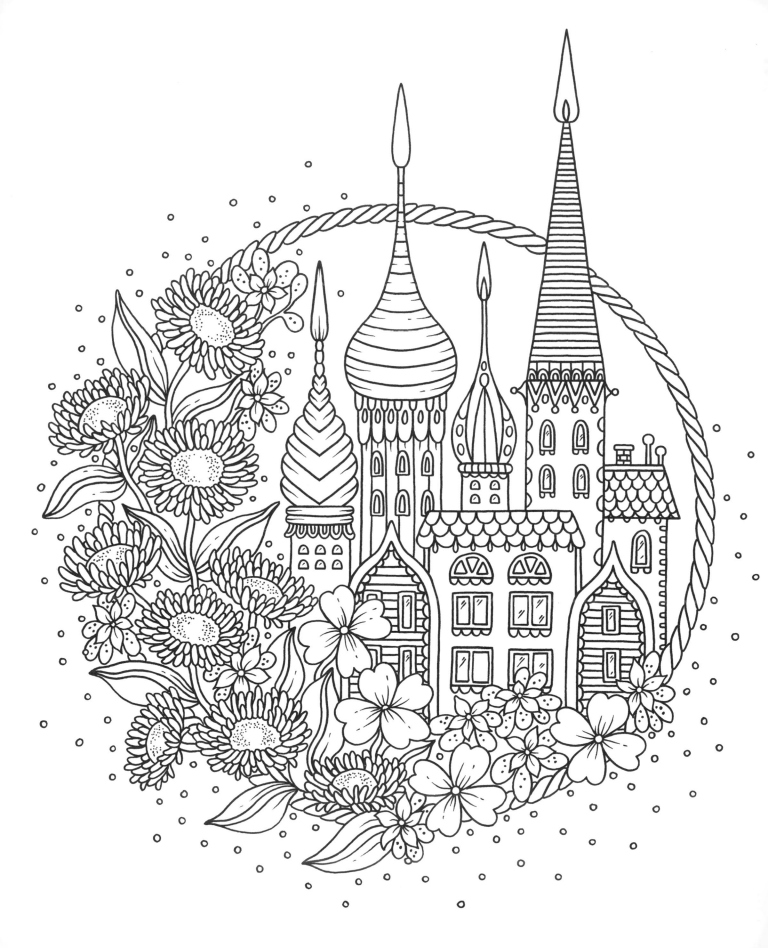

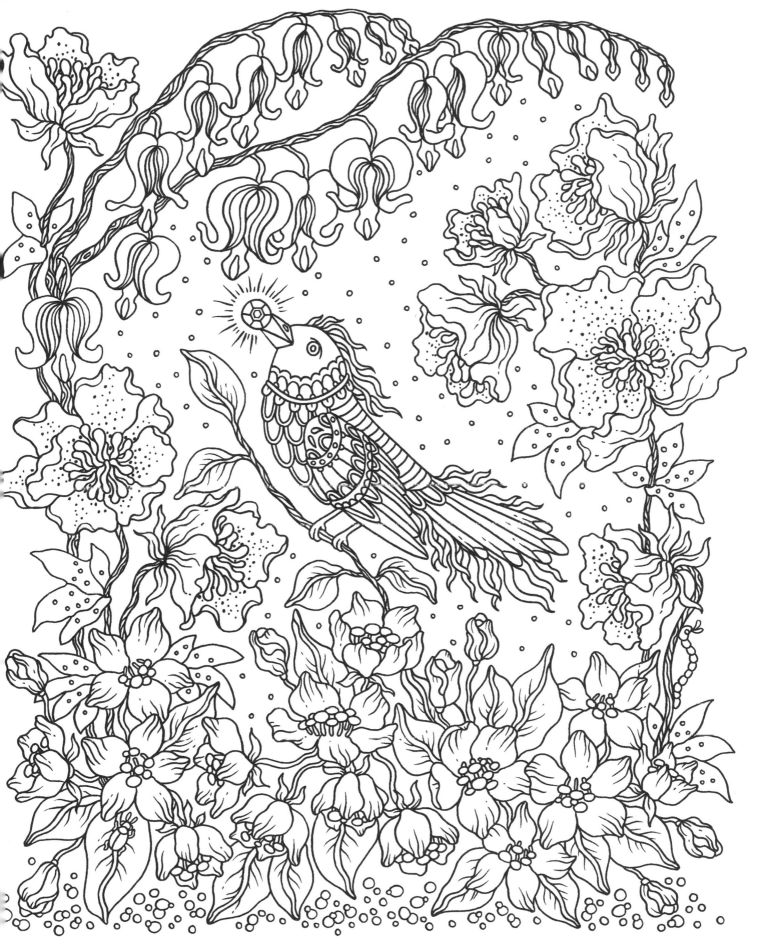

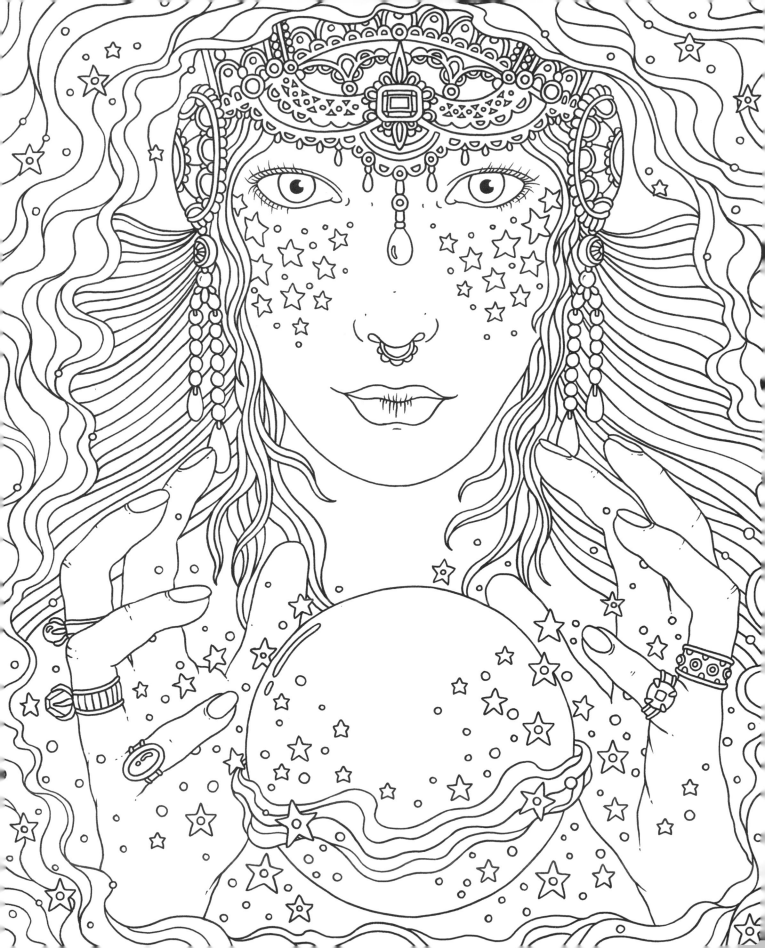

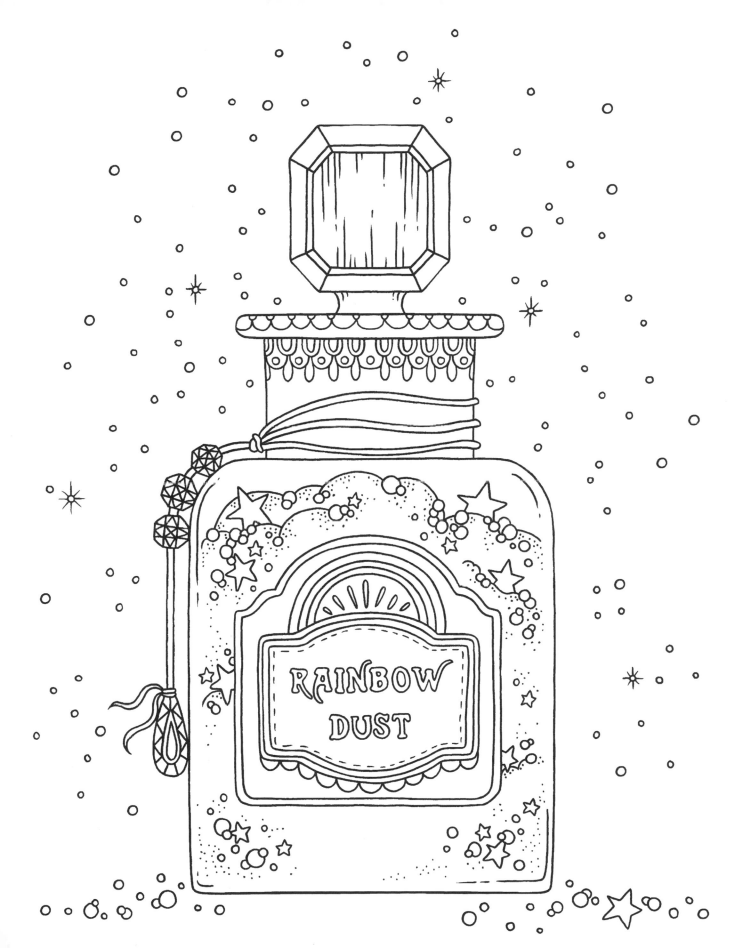

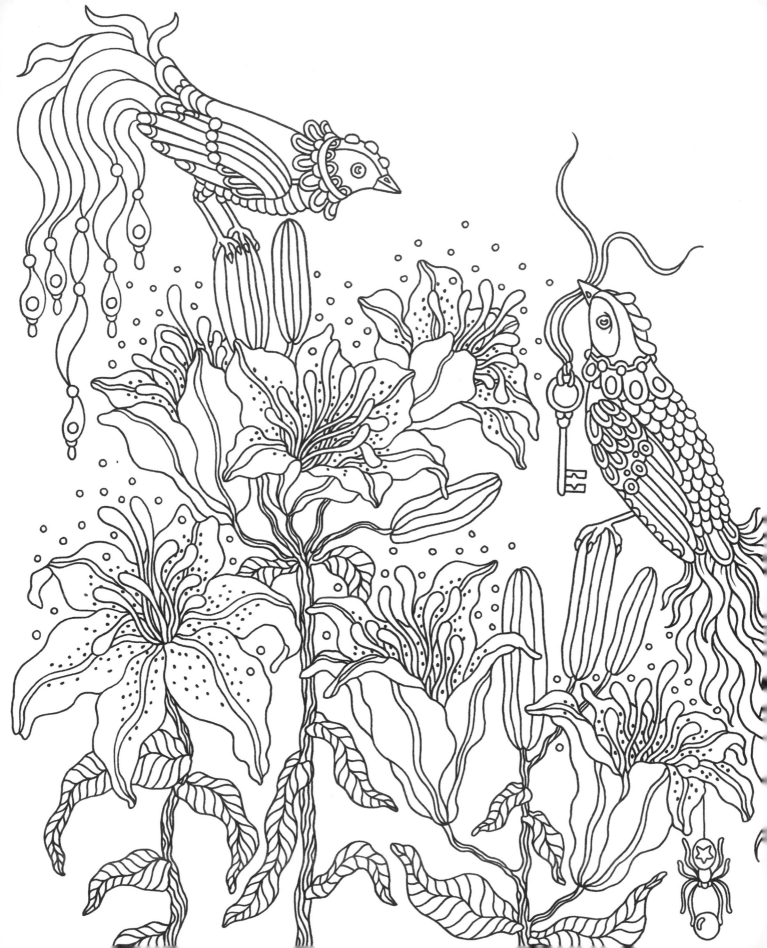

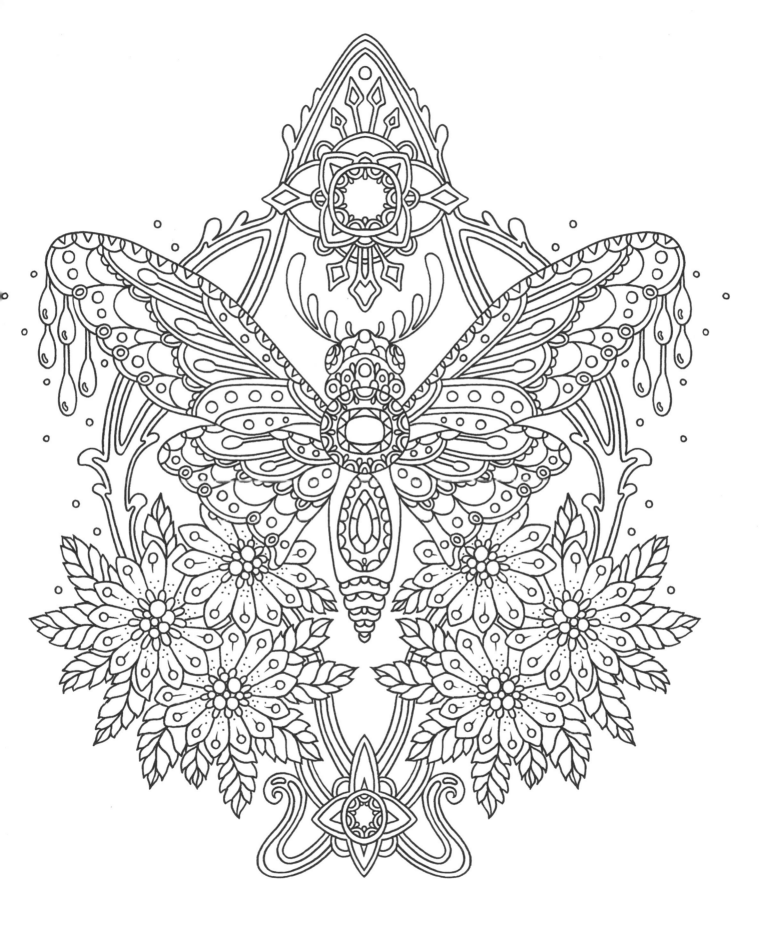

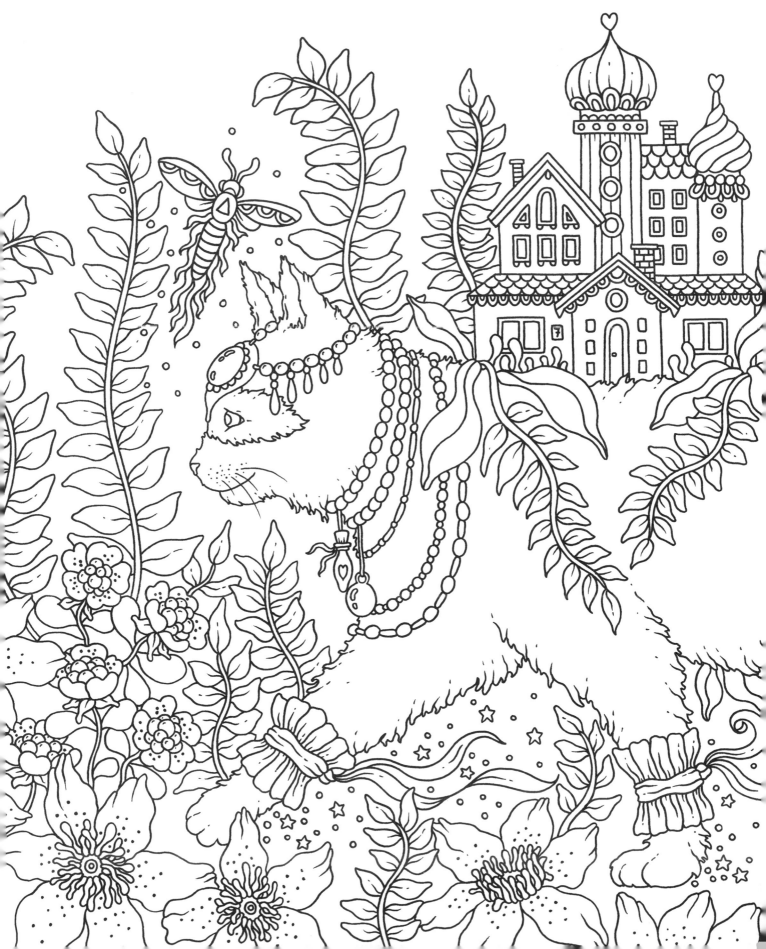

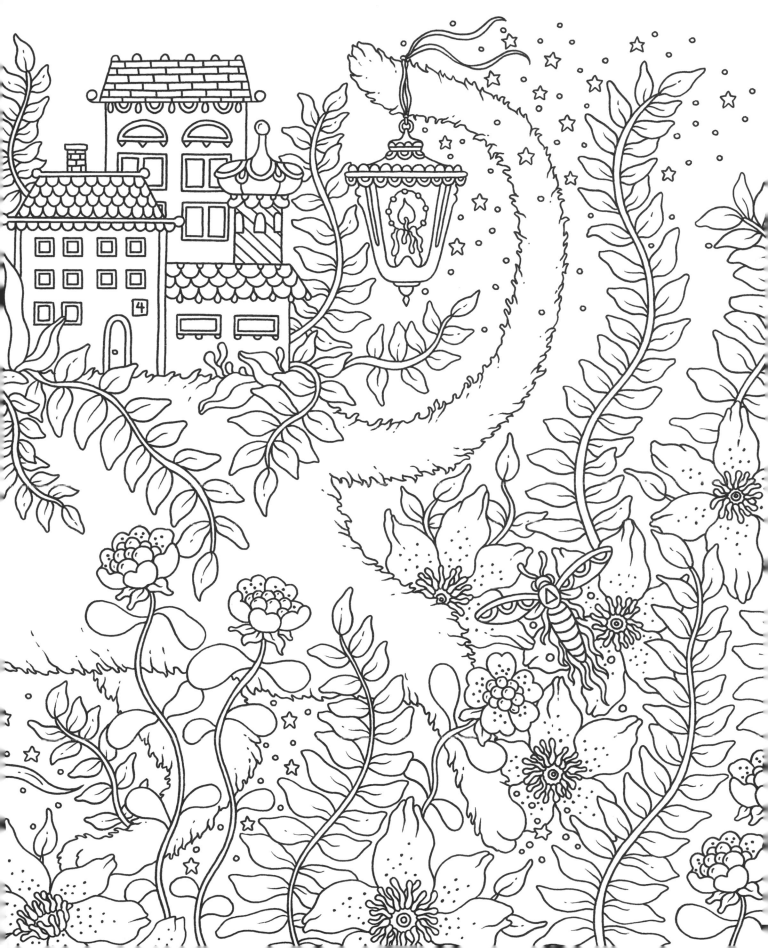

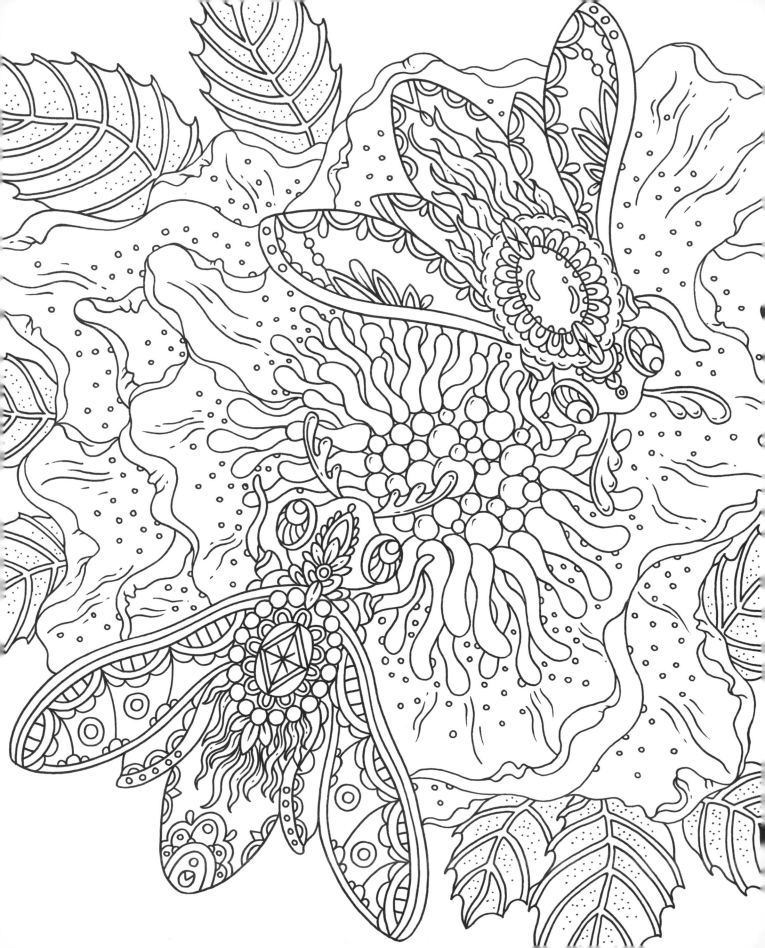

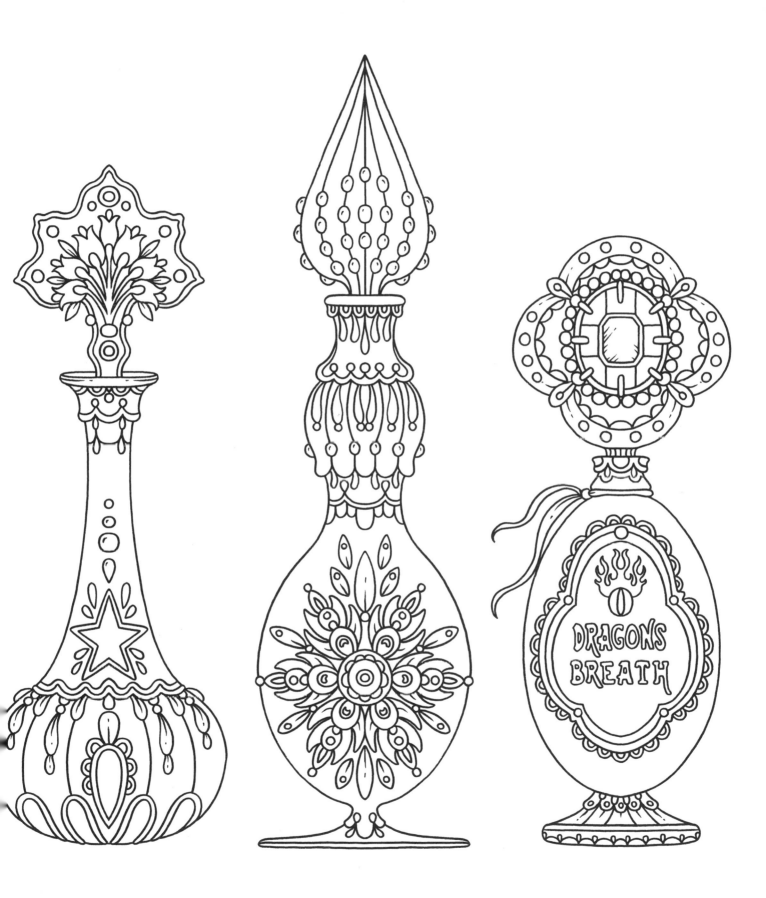

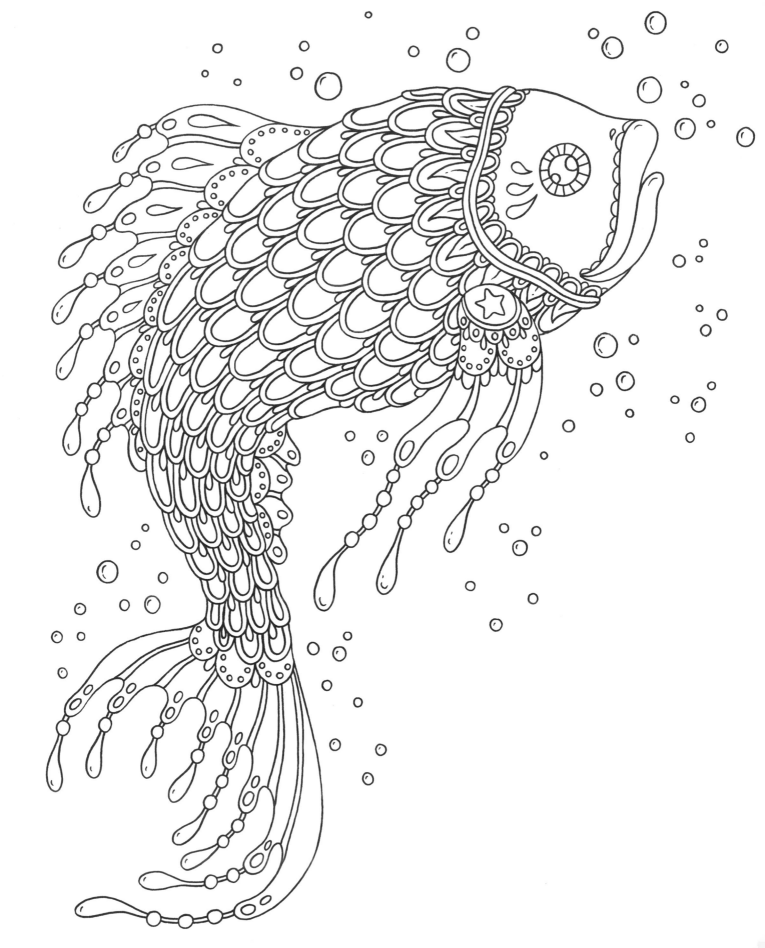

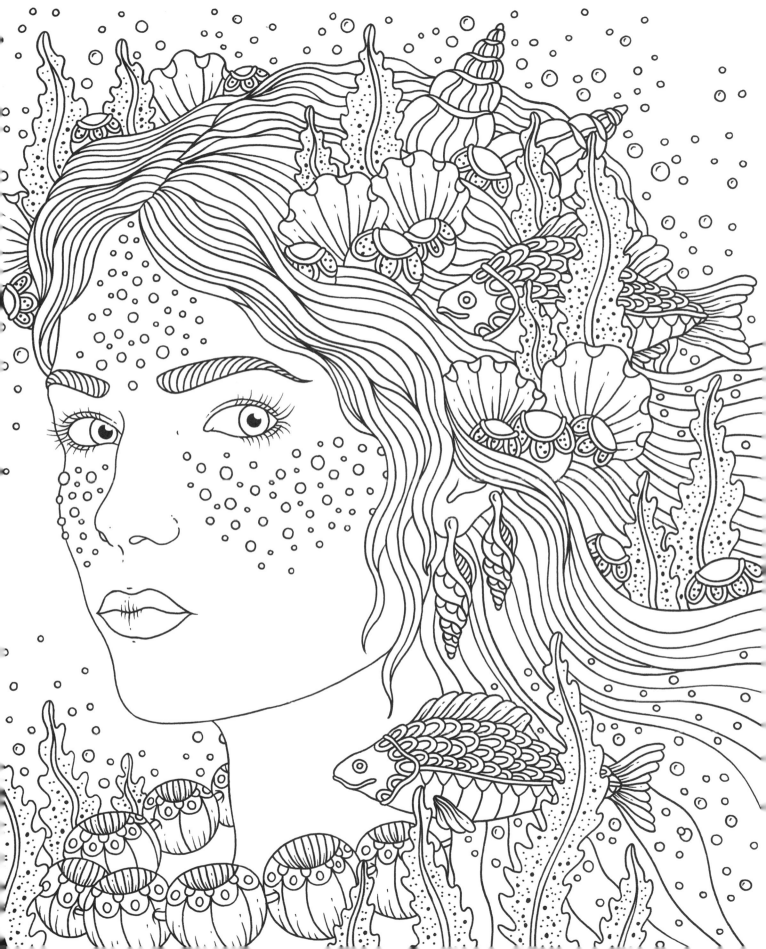

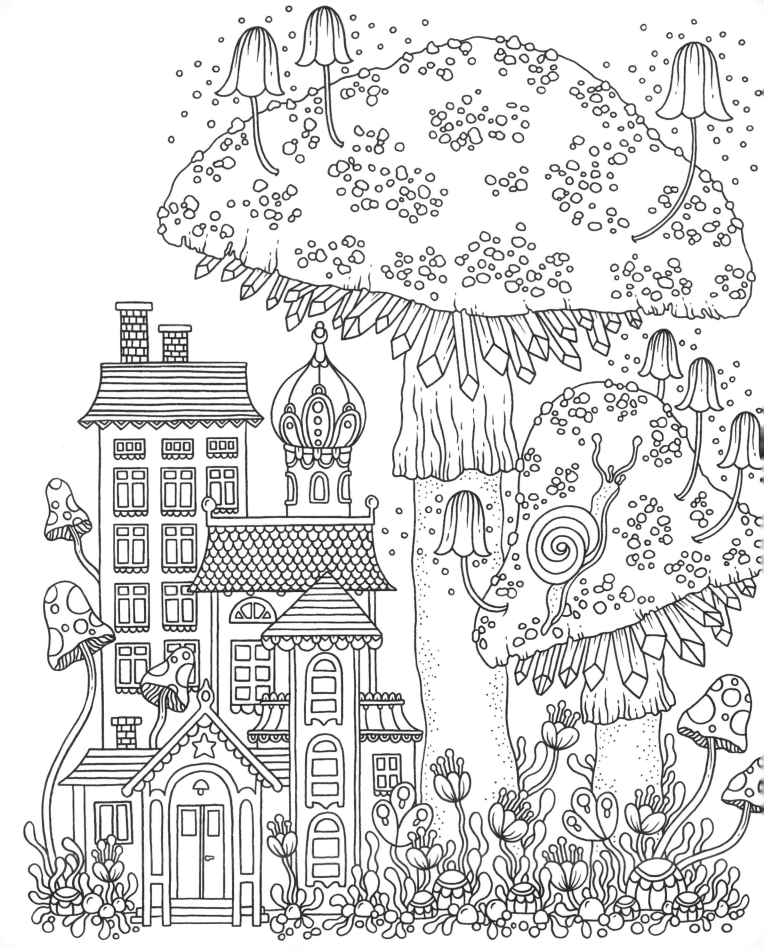

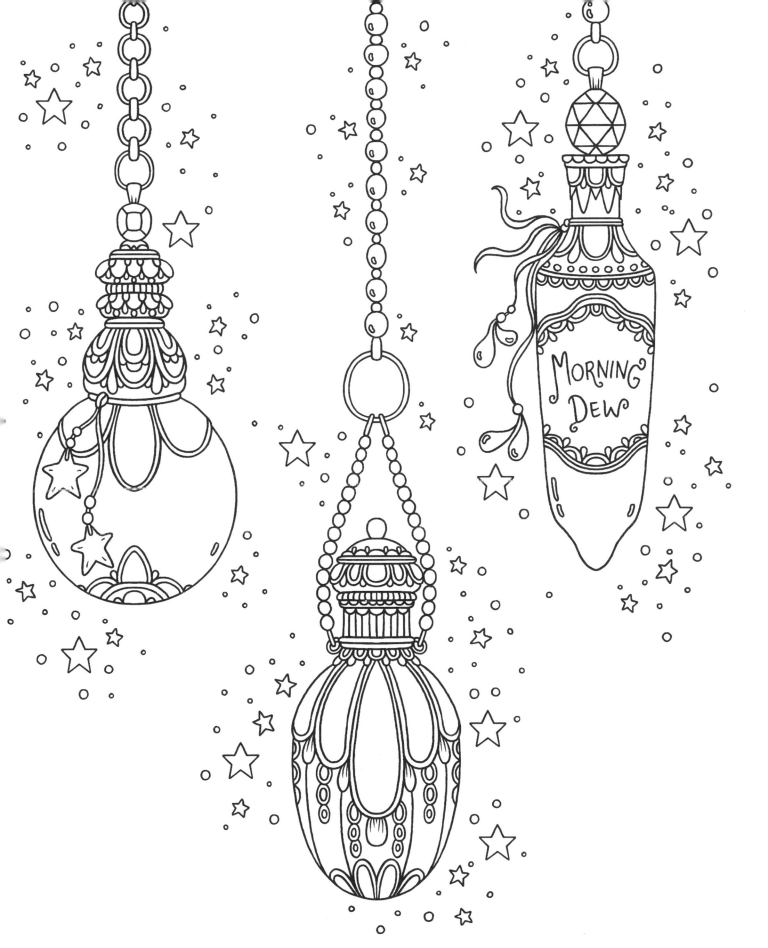

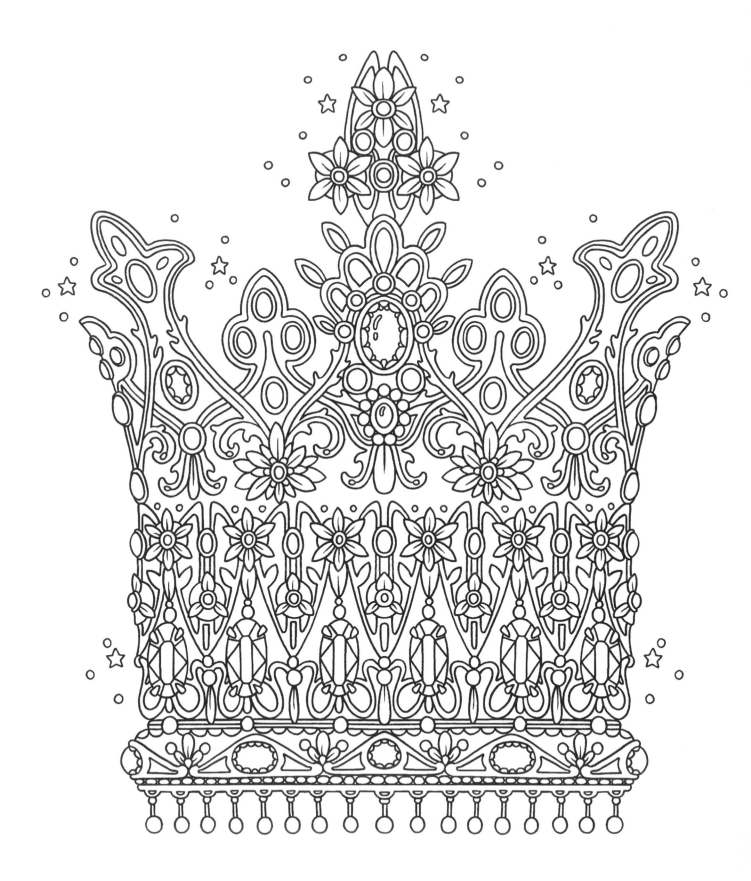

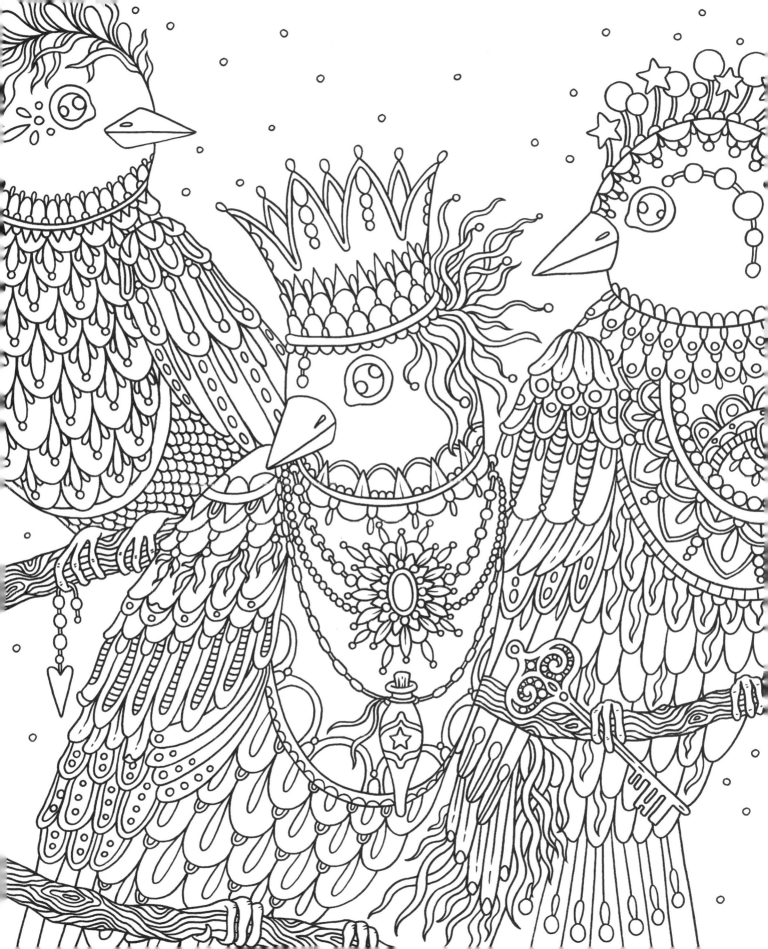

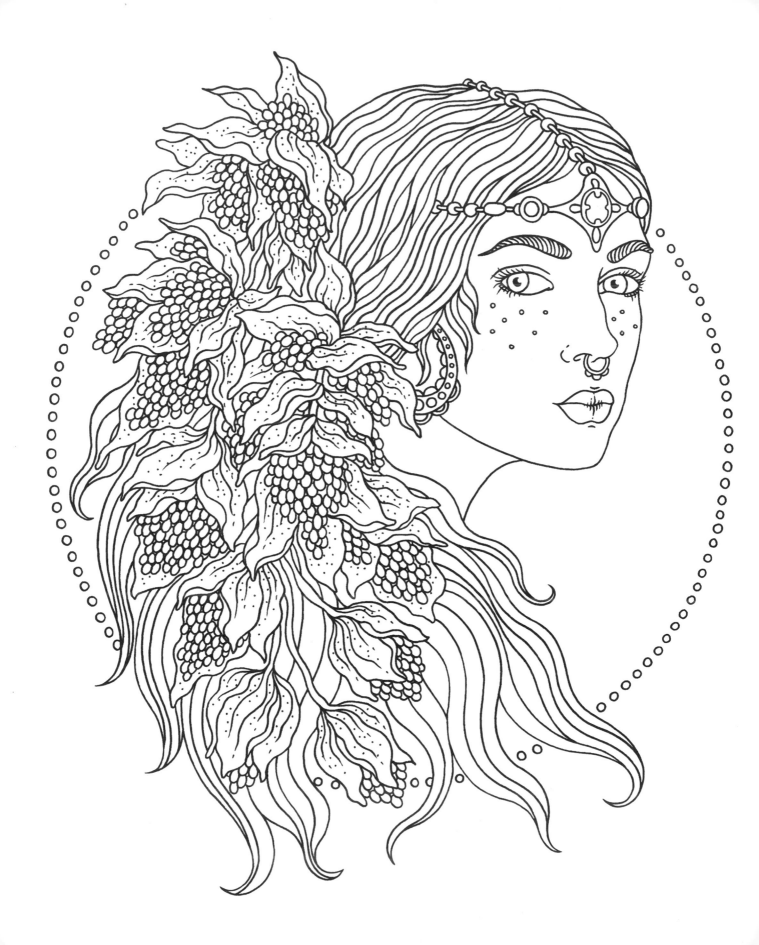

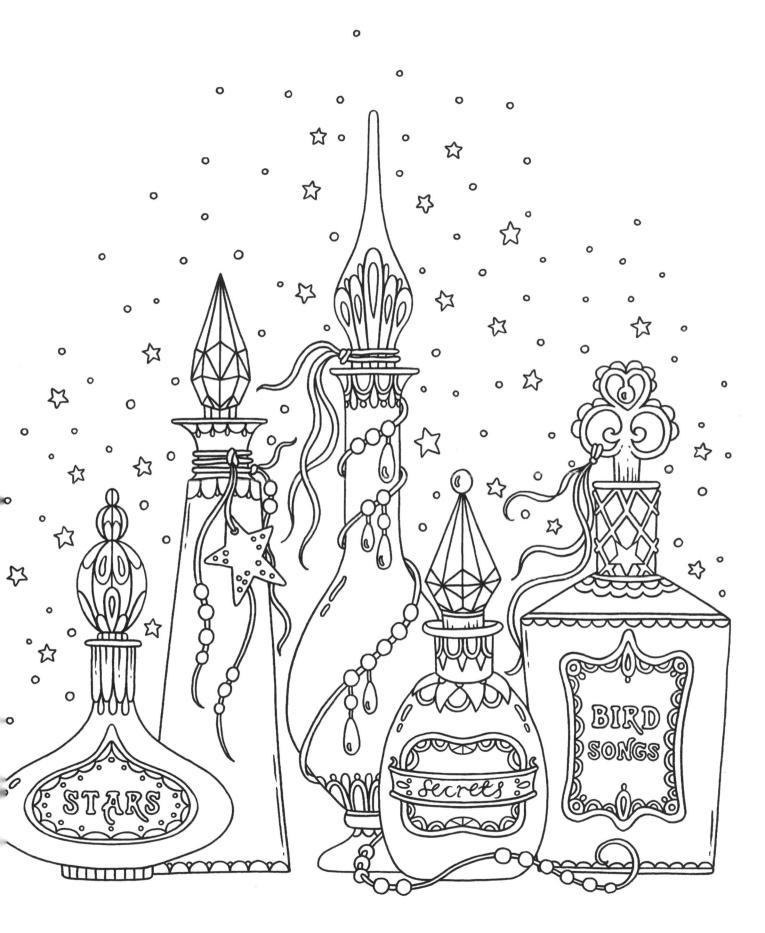

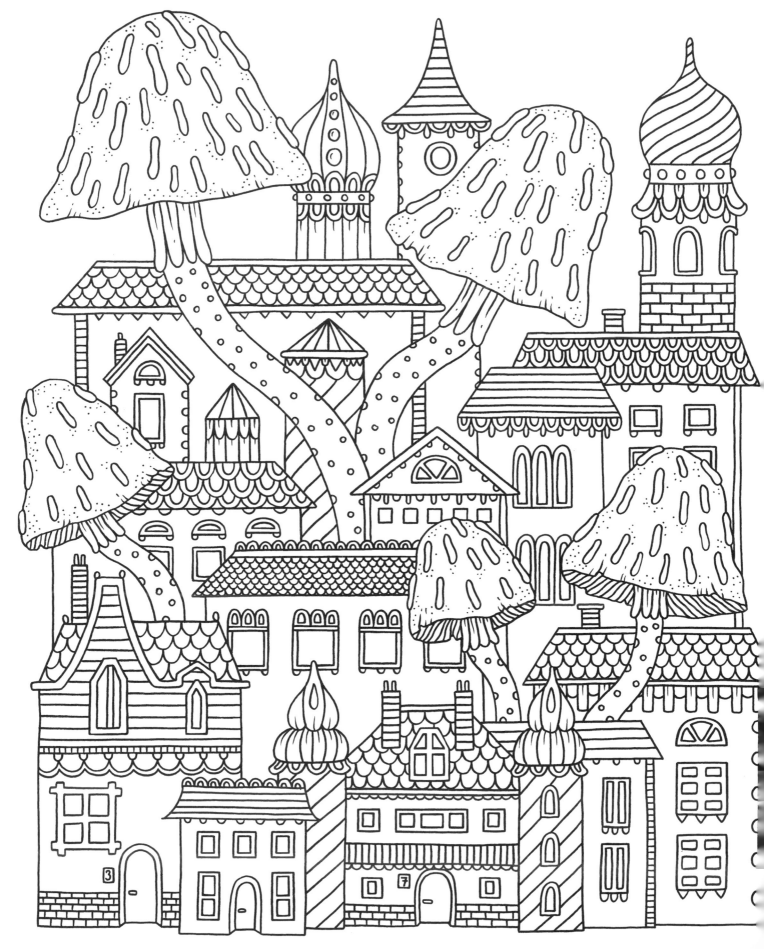

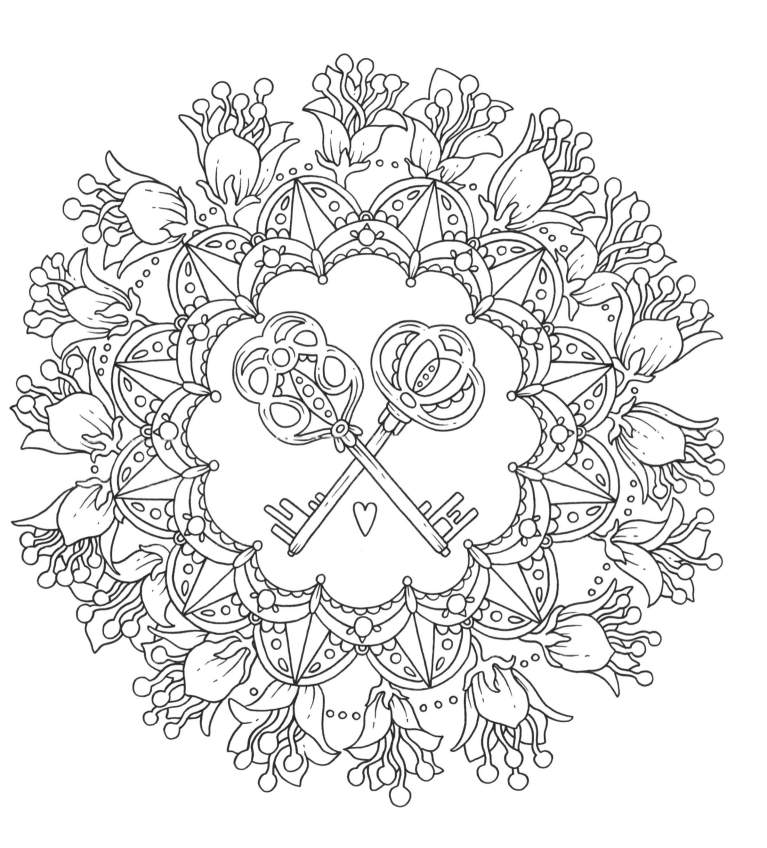

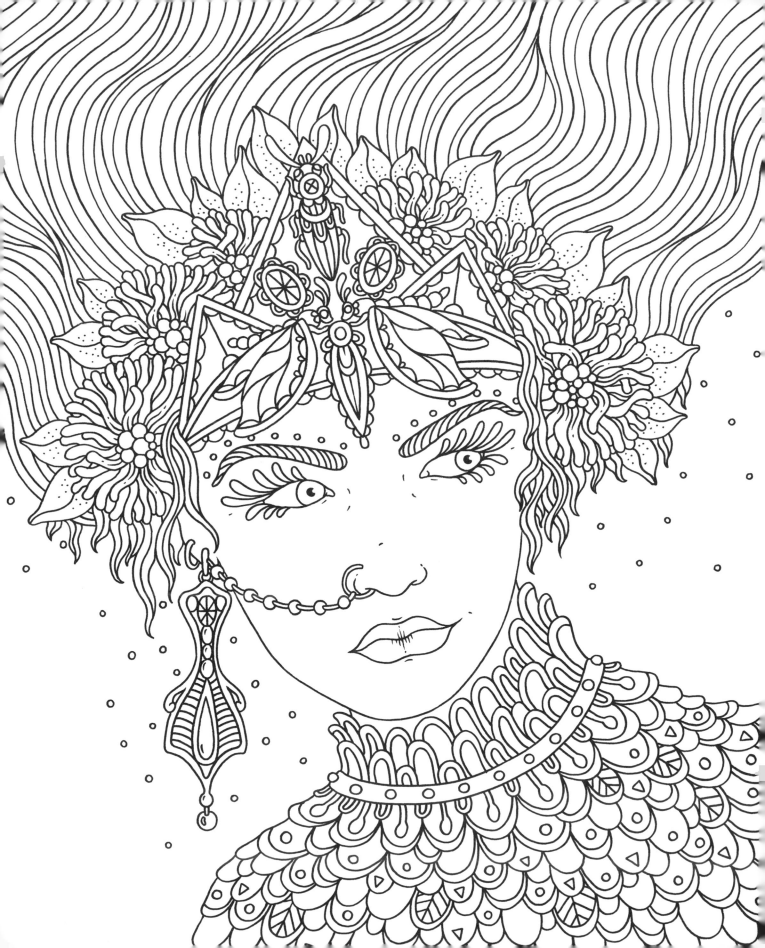

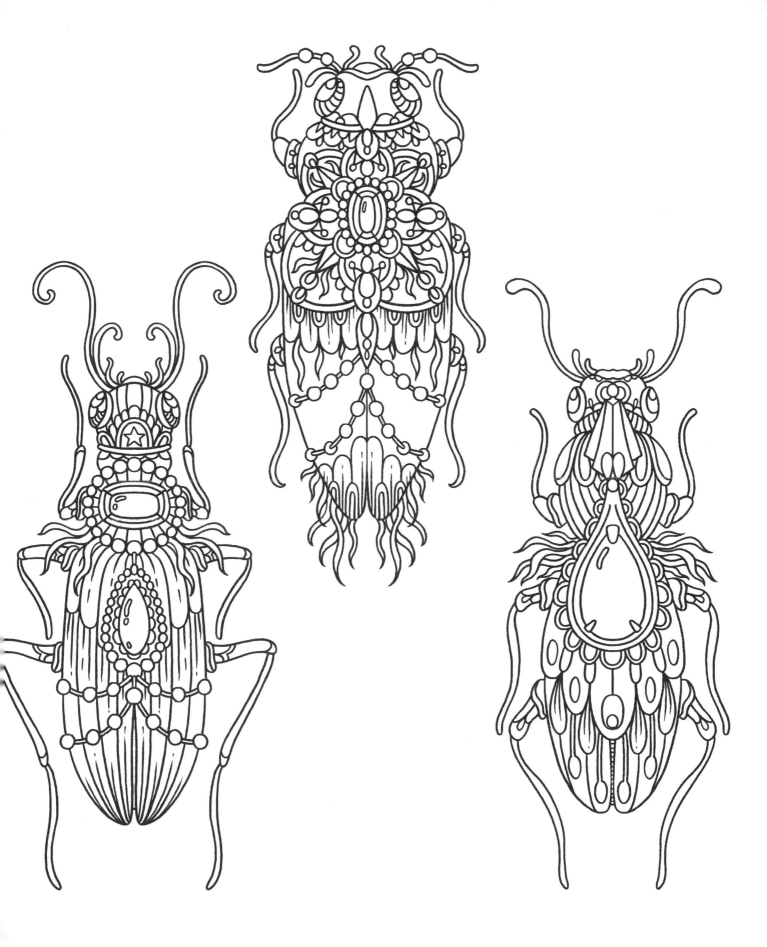

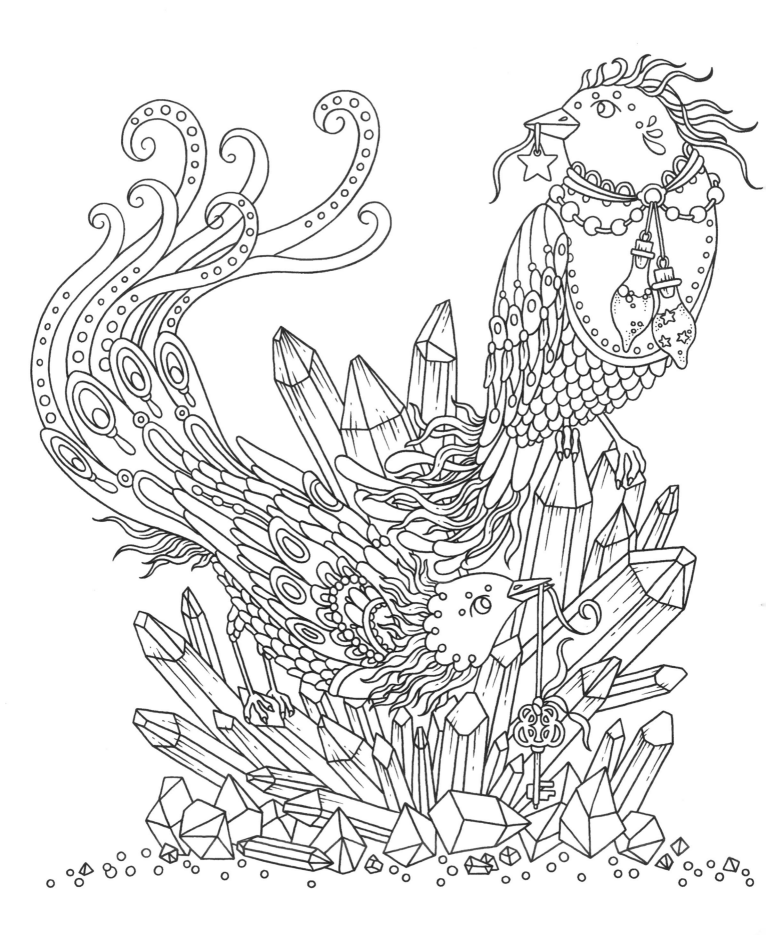

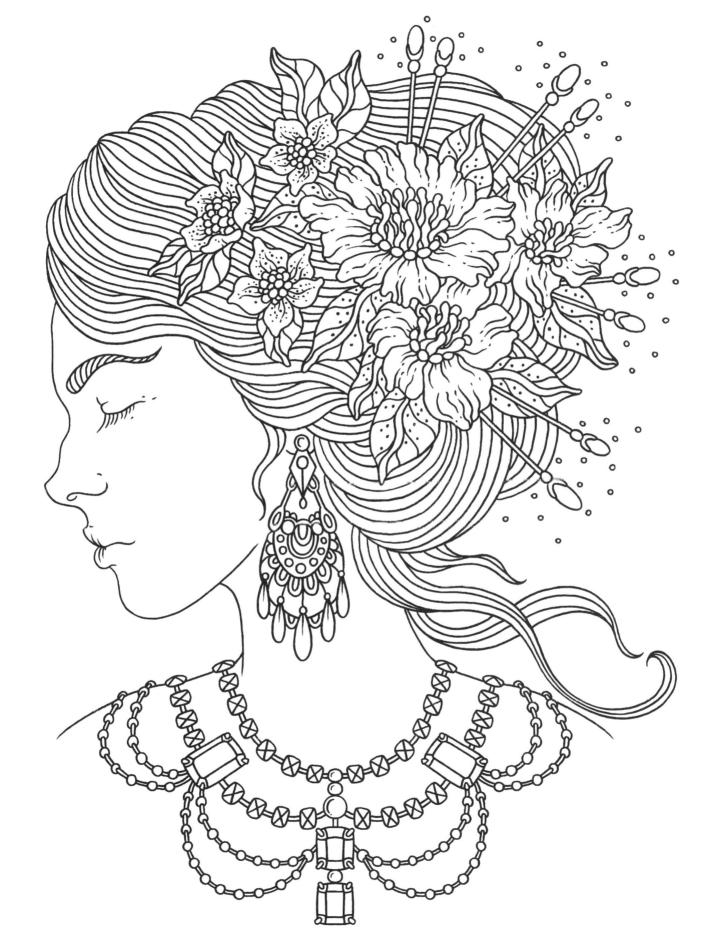

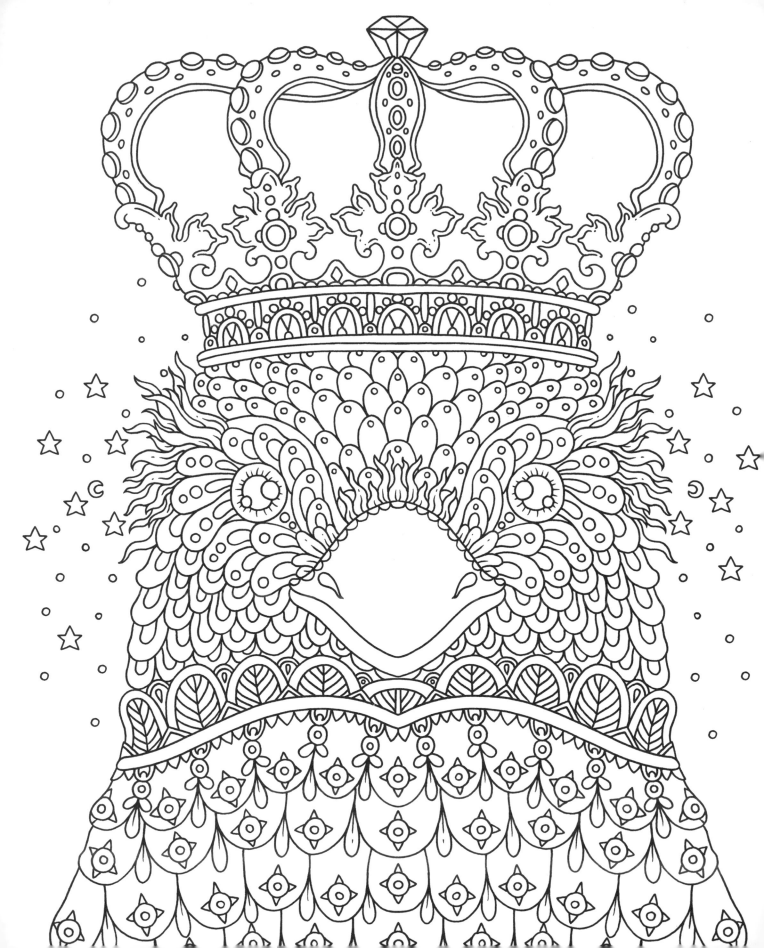

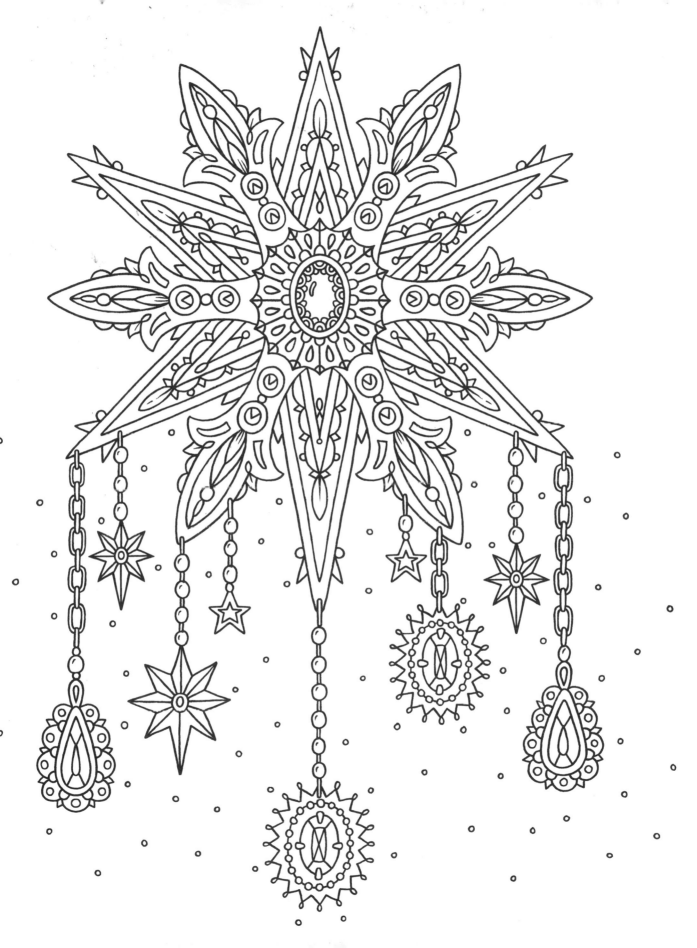

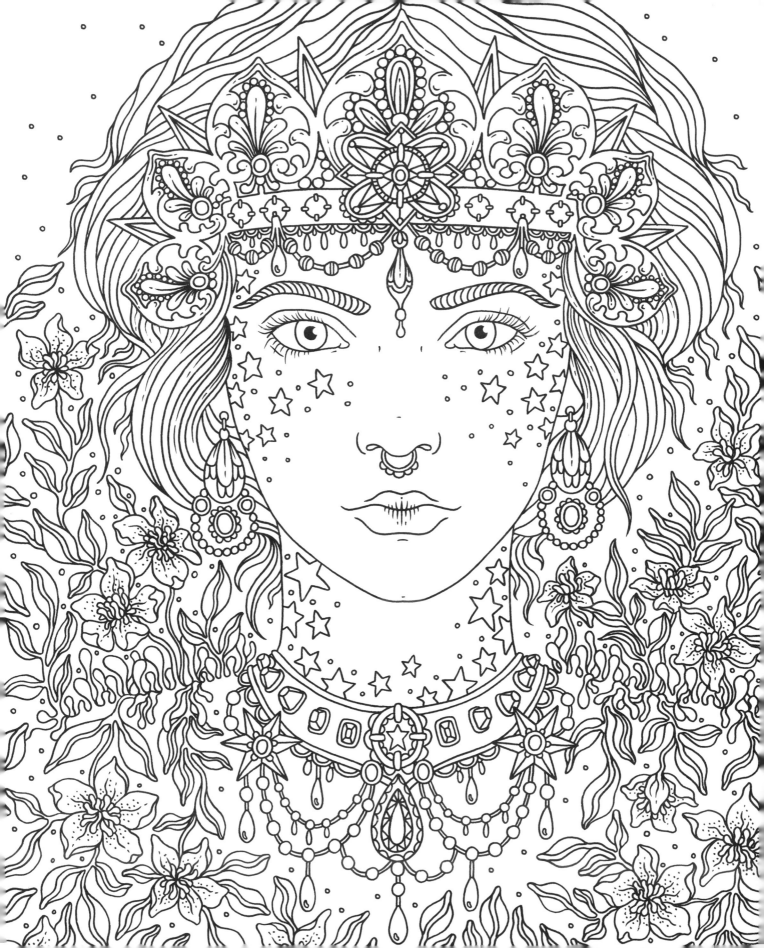

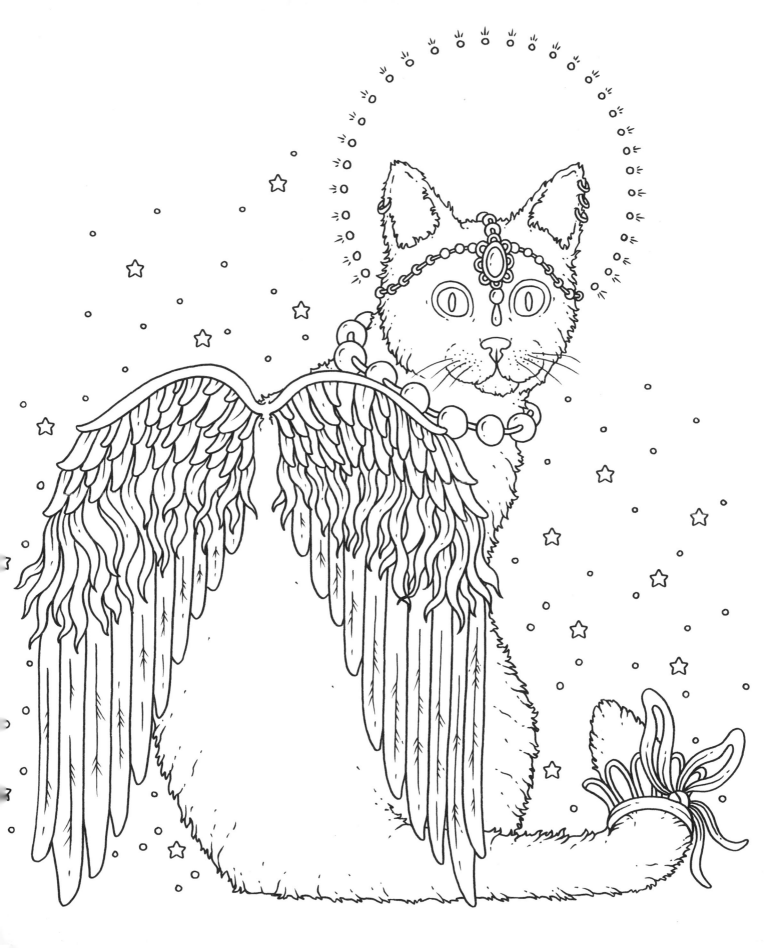

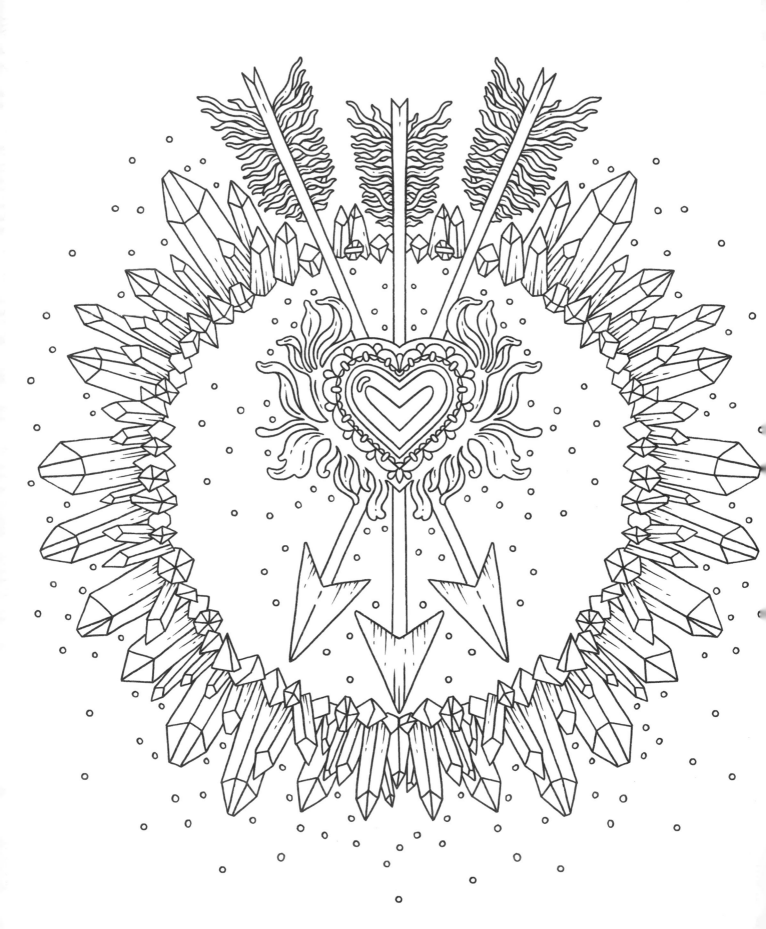

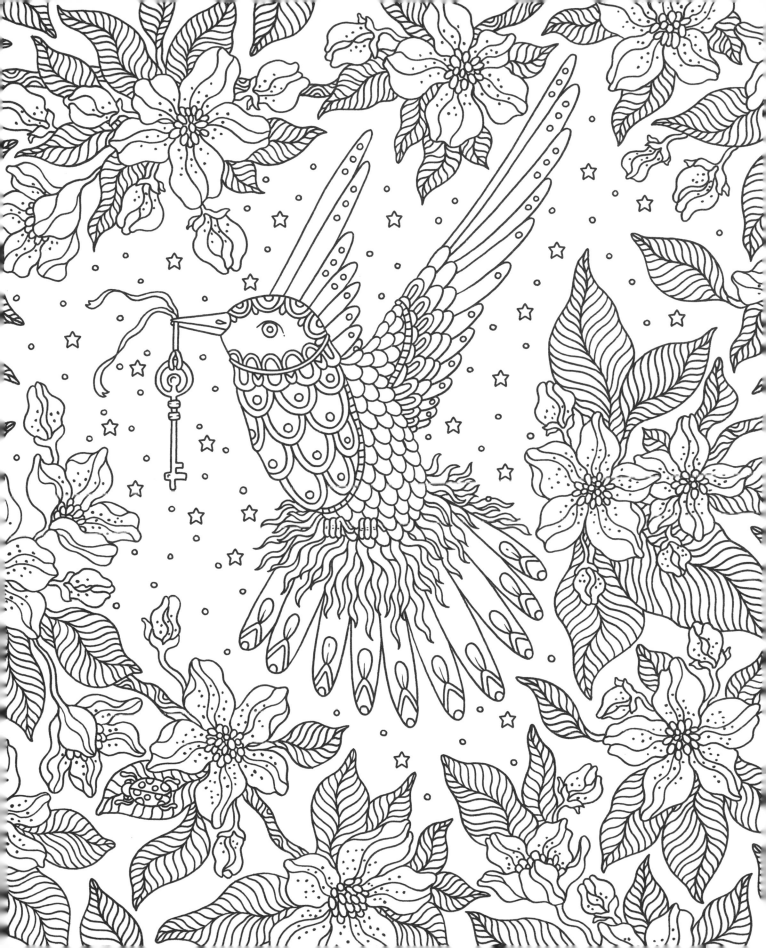

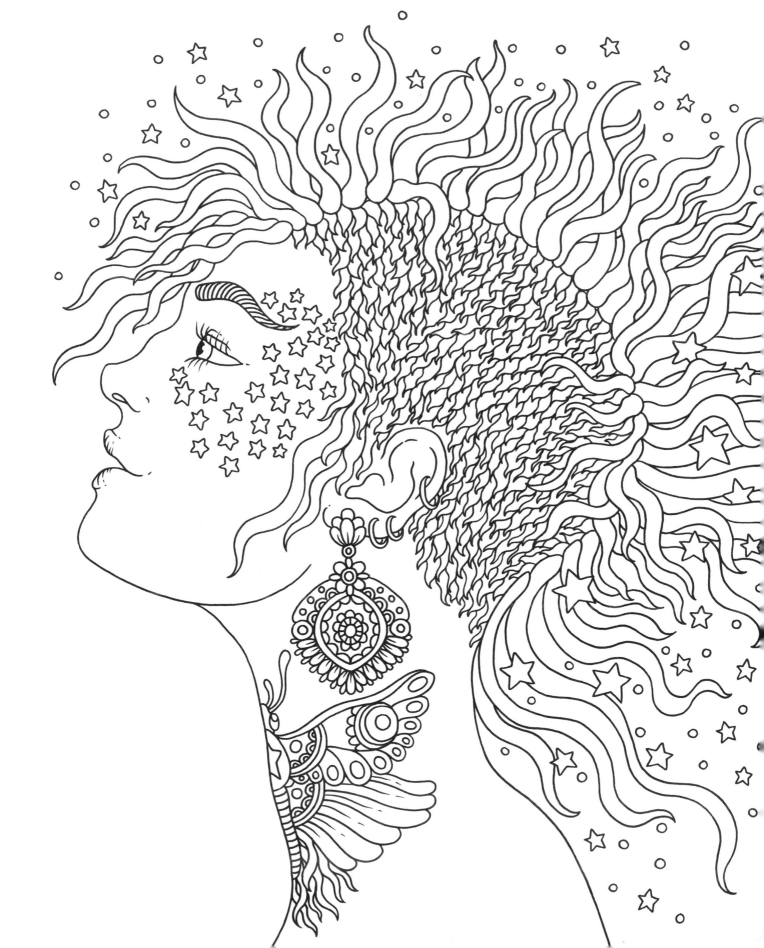

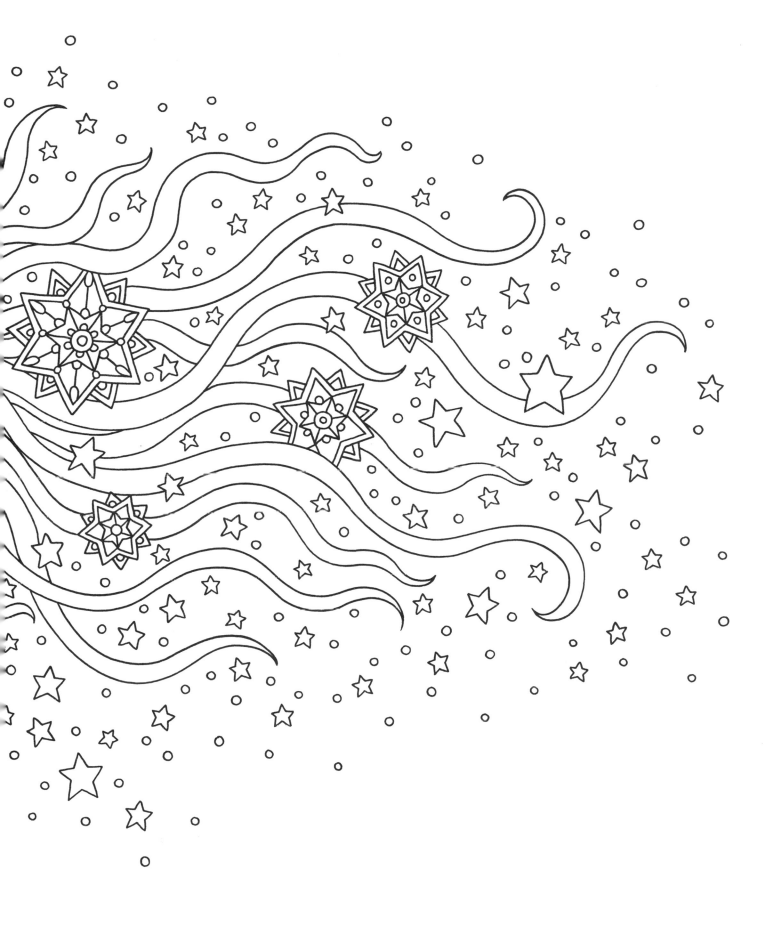

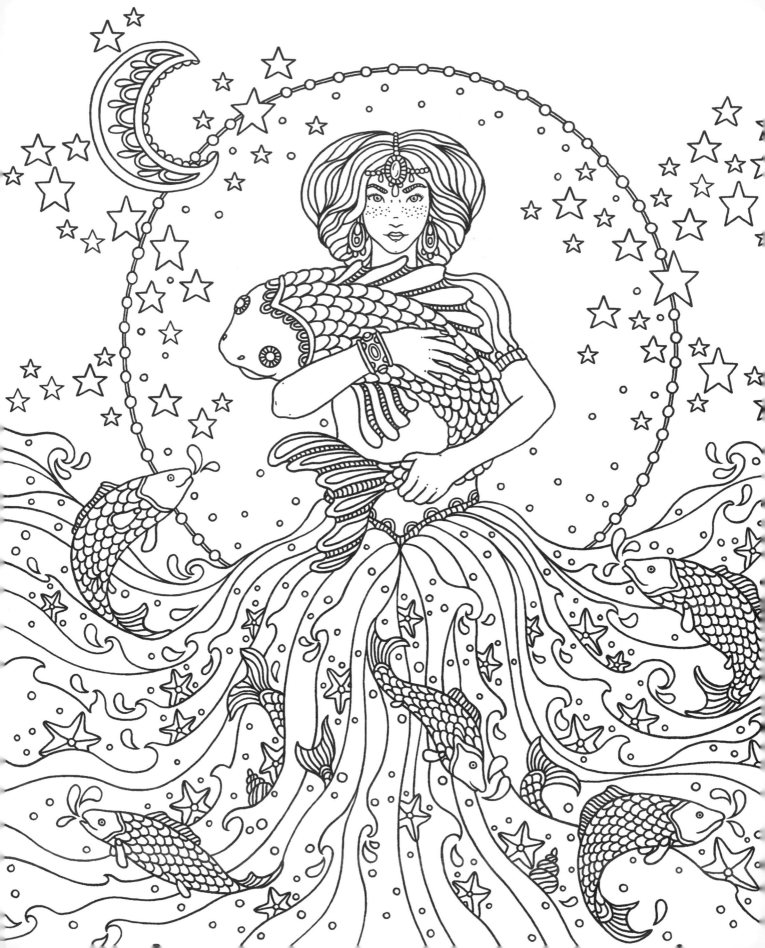

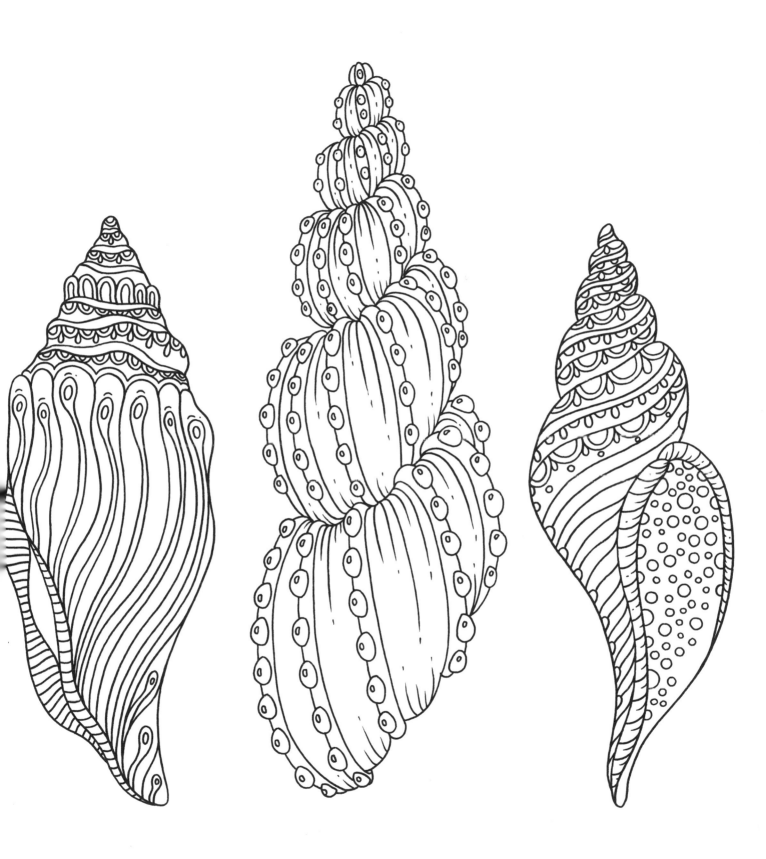

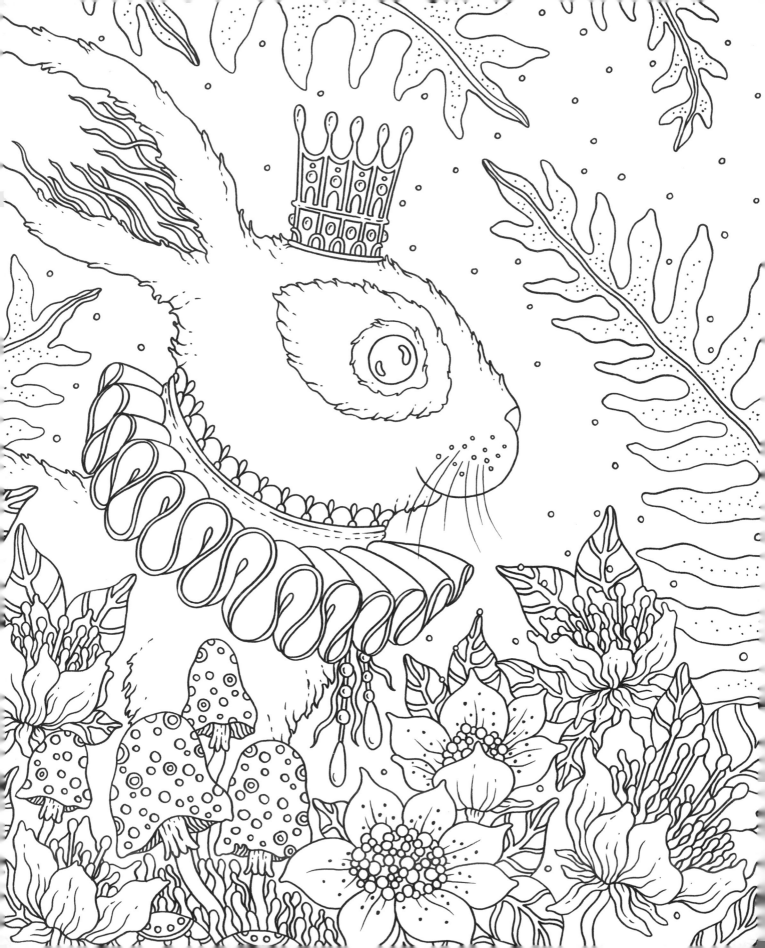

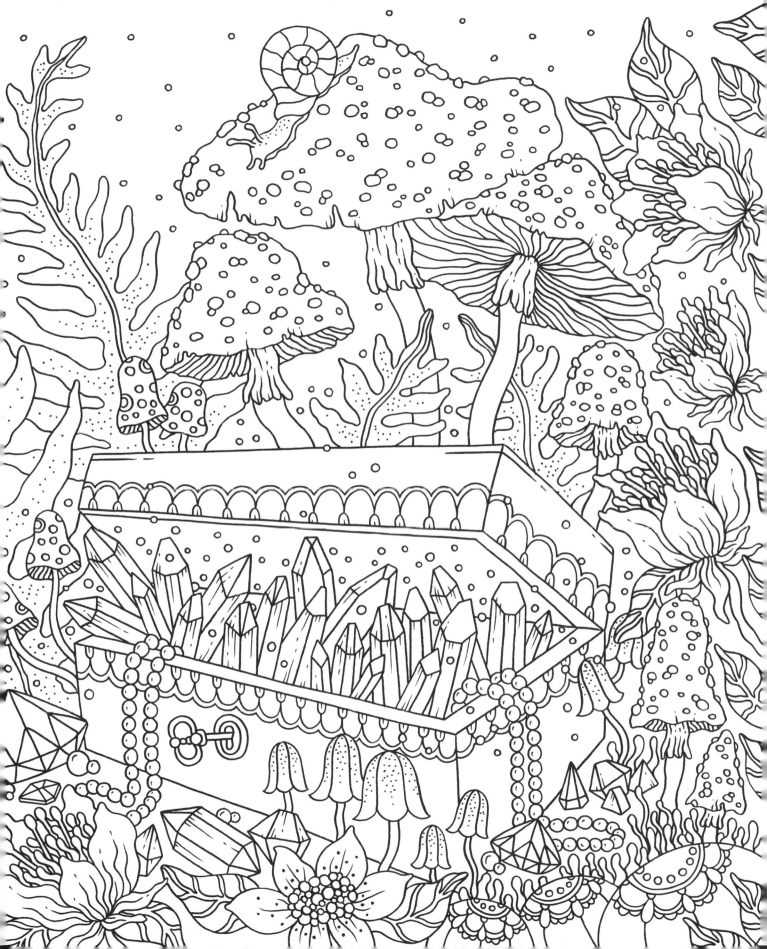

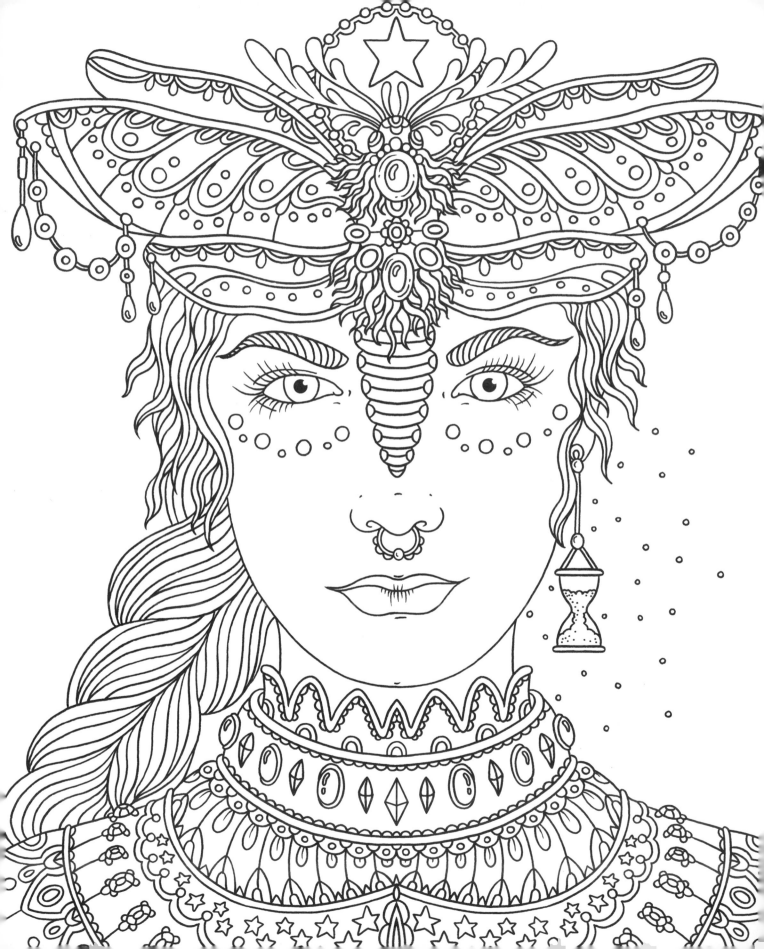

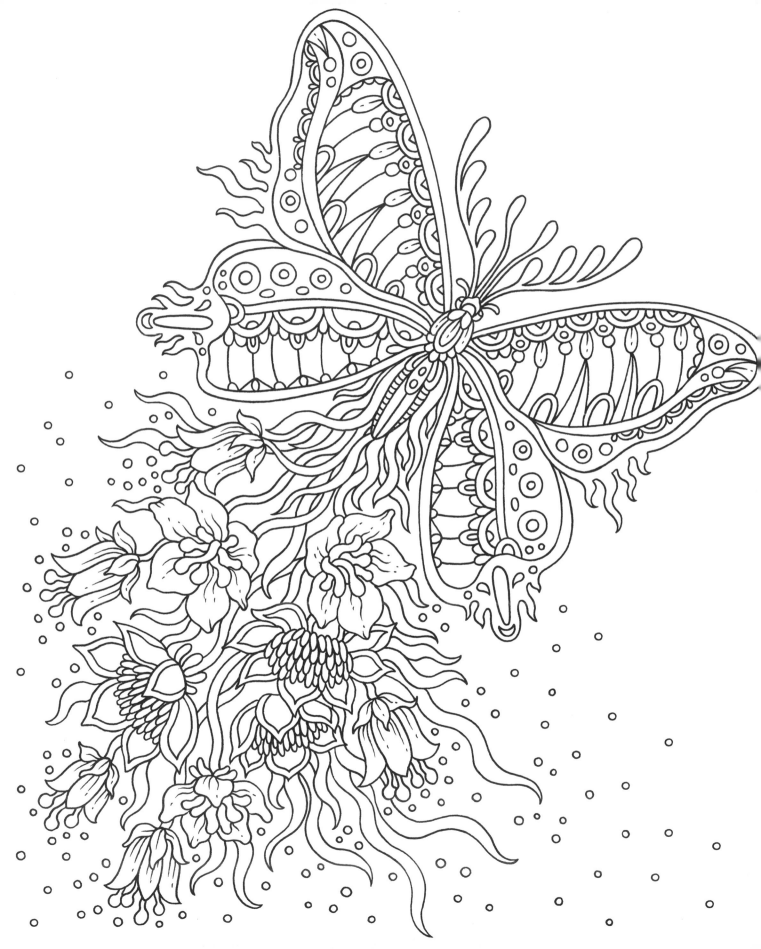

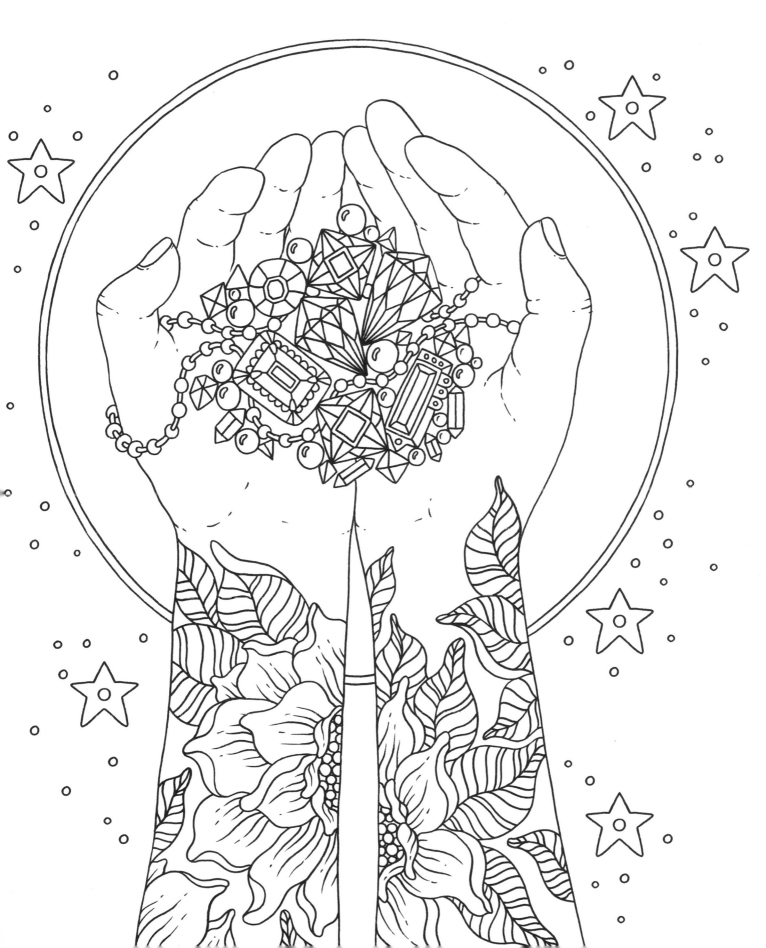

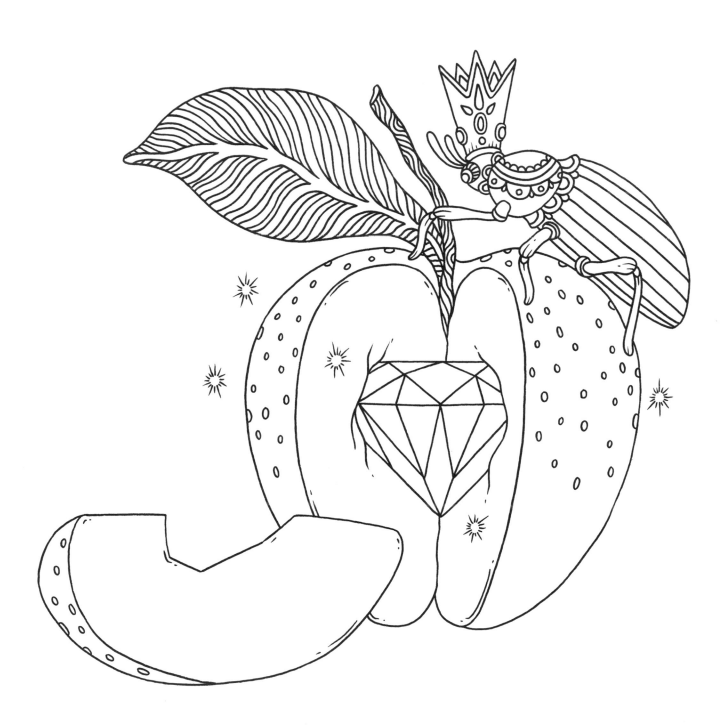